ConQuisTador of the UseleSS

JOSHUA ISARD

Conquistador of the Useless

JOSHUA ISARD

Cinco Puntos Press
EL PASO ★ TEXAS

Conquistador of the Useless
Copyright © 2013 by Joshua Isard

Printed in the United States.

First Edition
10 9 8 7 6 5 4 3 2 1

Library of Congress Cataloging-in-Publication Data

Isard, Joshua.
    Conquistador of the Useless / by Joshua Isard.—First Edition.
        pages cm
    ISBN 978-1-935955-54-2 (alk. paper), E-book ISBN 978-1-935955-55-9
    I. Title.

PS3609.S257C66 2013
813'.6--dc23

2012043175

Book and cover design by Anne Giangiulio.
Cover painting background by Bubba Haugh.
They're at it again!

CONTENTS

To my wife, Kate.

Alone, I might still be scribbling away about a certain Jonathan.
With you, I'm better.

"This music is the glue of the world.
It holds it all together."

—Empire Records

Scan below for a Spotify playlist of the music that accompanies
Conquistador of the Useless

1
HERE WE ARE NOW, ENTERTAIN US

My wife and I are on our way to eat dinner with people we
don't know. Apparently, this is what happens when you move
into an area where houses have lawns. The neighbors see you
directing the movers from the truck to your $300,000 storage
unit for boxes of stuff you suddenly wish you'd thrown out,
and they ask you what you're doing for dinner that night. Since,
you know, your kitchen won't be set up in the next few hours.

Because you're civilized, you understand it's unacceptable
to answer that you'd be happiest ordering a Papa John's and
watching your cats find ridiculous new hiding places. So you say,
Wow, I hadn't even thought about that, thanks for the offer.

That's why we're strolling down our driveway in whatever
outfits were on top of the suitcases we could reach among the
boxes. Lisa found a dress that didn't get too wrinkled, and I
pulled out a clean polo. We also discovered a bottle of Febreze,
which meant I didn't have to change my jeans.

Just food, my wife says, we eat and then we're gone.

We might like them, I say.

I can't imagine liking the kind of people who would
invite us into their home after knowing us for fifteen seconds.

If they'd spent any more time getting to know us, I
say, they wouldn't have invited us over. Besides, it was a nice
gesture.

She says, Do you remember when we were walking down 10th Street a little while ago and someone tapped you on the shoulder to tell you that your messenger bag's clasp was unfastened?

Yeah.

Do you remember what you said?

No.

You said, Why the fuck was that dude looking at my bag? Yeah, Nathan, you love nice gestures.

She's right about that. What I do like is grass. Grass between the sidewalk and the street, cleanly cut grass on each front lawn. And trees. Our new neighborhood's at the top of a hill, so when I look down it I see more trees than houses, more trees than streets or cars.

All that civilization is under the canopies somewhere, but from my perspective I can't see much of it.

I can, however, see my next-door neighbors' home as I approach it. I see their house-shaped mailbox which looks strikingly similar to their actual house, and which has The Harrison's hand painted on the little front door. That's a foreboding misuse of a possessive. But whatever, not a single car has come down the street during our short walk, and that's a decent trade.

Tom Harrison and I are barbecuing in his back yard while our wives make the pasta salad in the kitchen. Couples, when put together in an uncontrolled environment, split up along the lines of a middle school dance.

As Tom flips burgers I realize how much taller I am than him, mostly because I'm not that tall. It's rare that I have a head on someone. I stick my hands in my pockets and watch him grill, resist the urge to tell him not to press down on the patties since it dries them out, and also see how much stockier he is than me. I can't tell if he's fat or just bulky. I feel like he and Kristy may have asked us over as much because they think we're too thin as to be neighborly.

Tom asks me if I barbecue a lot.

I might now, I say, but I couldn't do much of it in our place downtown.

Well, you might want to look into one of these bad boys, he says as he steps back and looks over his six burner gas grill. I could cook for the whole block on this thing.

He waves at the machine with an oversized spatula made of industrial strength stainless steel, one with serrated edges that make it look more like a torture device than a utensil.

Cool, I say, but I have an old Weber that ought to do for us.

Yeah, he says, but how many people can you have over with an old Weber?

It seems odd to say that we don't want to have a lot of people over, so I just tell him that's a good point.

Then he asks me what I do, so I talk about being an office manager for Toaner Optic Networks, and he says he knows the company because his agency found Toaner the real estate for its warehouse.

What a coincidence, he says.

Yeah, I say.

I don't mention that I've never been to the warehouse, that I didn't even know we had a new one until I got an email telling me to change some addresses, that what happens there has almost nothing to do with my running the offices. Maybe I should, because as Tom flips the burgers he has a satisfied grin on his face like he's started planning our man dates for the next few months.

~

We sit down to eat at the table on their patio, and I get to spend time with my wife again on one of the more momentous days of our marriage.

Kristy, you won't believe it, Tom says, but Nate here works for Toaner, that company I worked on the warehouse deal for a few years ago.

Really, she says. And she's genuinely surprised, as if she found out I owned the company.

Yeah, I say, it's true.

I put my hand on Lisa's knee, and she smiles, but it's that smile which I know means she's not at all happy.

So, Kristy says, how long have you been married?

Four years, Lisa answers.

That's wonderful, Kristy says, we've been married almost eight years now.

She says it like they'd beaten us at some contest.

Tom then picks up the bowl of pasta salad, which I take as a sign that we can all start eating, so I pass the little basket of hamburger buns to Lisa. This starts the carousel of plates, and after it circles the table we all have burgers, coleslaw, corn on the cob, and a very spicy pasta salad.

Somebody has to say something at a meal like this, and they usually do when everyone else has their mouth full. So, just as I take a large bite of my burger, and Lisa starts chewing a forkful of coleslaw, Kristy asks us if we're originally from the area.

Then we have the awkward seconds where Tom and his wife watch us chew, and Lisa and I look at each other to see who's going to be done first.

It's me.

Yeah, I say, we both grew up around here. We were actually wondering the other day if we chose this neighborhood because it reminds us of when our biggest concern was keeping our Nirvana CDs from getting scratched.

Tom asks, You're Nirvana fans?

Yeah, I say, who wasn't growing up in the '90s, right?

Remind me to show you something after we're done with dinner.

All right, I say.

We all resume eating and after a while I feel like it's my responsibility to break the tension of four people trying not to be heard chewing.

I really like the pin oak in your back yard, Tom and Kristy. It's gorgeous. Must look amazing when the colors change in the fall.

They look at me, a little confused. So does Lisa, actually.

Oh, Tom says, the big one in the middle of the yard?

Yeah.

We were actually thinking about getting rid of that, freeing up some lawn space.

Oh, I say.

But, Kristy says, it is beautiful in the fall.

Now I'm hoping they wait a few years so I can see it change while I sit in my own yard.

After we eat dessert I'm in Tom's home office upstairs while Kristy and Lisa have a cup of tea. I'd tell Tom that I love relaxing with a cup of tea after dinner, but that might ruin our guy thing happening right now.

He walks me to the back of the room where there's a white guitar mounted on the wall, behind glass.

This is what I wanted to show you, he says.

Oh.

It's a Fender Jaguar. See who signed it?

Some scribbles around the bridge look like they could be words from any western language.

I tell him that I can't make out the signatures.

It's Kurt Cobain, Krist Novoselic and Dave Grohl. Cobain played this exact guitar during a concert at the Spectrum in 1992.

No fucking way.

Yeah. Kristy got this for me on our anniversary last year. Nirvana's always meant a lot to me, you know?

I don't, but I let him talk about it.

When Smells Like Teen Spirit came out, he says, I wasn't a popular guy. I wasn't after it came out either, but that song made me realize I wasn't the only one who thought all the cliques and fashion and what not at my school was bullshit.

Yeah, I say. And now, twenty years later, you've got this.

We can afford it. Kristy's an anesthesiologist, and I already told you I'm in real estate, so this guitar ends up being a nice treat. A little validation, maybe.

He's definitely bulky, I think to myself, not fat. I can see him at a gym, bench pressing, thinking about all the cool kids who spurned him as he goes for that last rep.

I don't want this to turn into a conversation about how we like Nirvana, because my favorite one of their songs is Son of a Gun, a nonsense B-side cover.

So I ask, Are you a Pixies fan?

A little, he says.

It's just, that's why I got into Nirvana when I was a teenager, because they sounded like Pixies.

Tom doesn't seem impressed. I'm back in high school, trying to be a legit fan, someone who knew about them early, only now I don't have a faded concert t-shirt to prove my point.

There's a cool story behind the title, Smells Like Teen Spirit, I say. Kurt Cobain's girlfriend, the singer from Bikini Kill, wrote, Kurt smells like teen spirit! on the wall of his bedroom, and she thought it was funny because Teen Spirit was a brand of deodorant for girls.

What?

Shit. He looks like a ten-year-old who just figured out he's never going to play big league baseball.

That's where the title comes from, I say. Just a little trivia.

Interesting, he says.

Somebody mowed their lawn that evening, because I get the cut grass smell during our walk home. That's enough to make me love our decision to move.

Why did you leave me with her? Lisa asks.

You think I wanted to? Nate, come help with the burgers, Nate let me show you my Nirvana guitar. I hate it when people call me Nate.

Wait, what Nirvana guitar?

Kristy didn't tell you? Tom has a guitar signed by all the members of Nirvana. He told me about how Smells Like Teen Spirit changed his life in high school.

Oh, Jesus…

I know. But, I think I ruined his whole idea of that song when I told him about what that punk singer wrote on Kurt Cobain's wall.

Kathleen Hanna?

Yeah. I told Tom about that. I think it took some of the impact away.

Well, Lisa says, at least you didn't talk about travel. Kristy asked me about our honeymoon, so I told her about Japan and everything, but then she wouldn't stop talking about her and Tom's trip to Italy.

We met these people today and you already talked about honeymoons?

Hey, you talked about his boyhood insecurities.

Fair enough.

So, Lisa says, Kristy asked me if I'd been to Rome and Florence and all the places they went. So I told her about that Italian wine tour I went on, and she says something like, Oh, well Tom and I didn't drink while we were over there.

What?

Yeah. Kristy said, That way we saved money, and stayed hydrated.

Shit, I say.

I open the door and we walk into this Tetris game of our new living room and sigh.

Lisa says, We won't see the cats for three days.

I'll bet they're having a blast.

In the back yard—the cleanest part of my new property—the light's fading from deep orange to dark blue. When the breeze blows, the last bits of pale sunlight slip through some leaves and hit my lawn.

I'm sitting on a folding chair I brought out to my own patio—we haven't bought outdoor furniture yet. Instead of a fence, my half-acre back yard has spruces along the property line, which means that I can't see much into the adjacent yards, and my neighbors can't see any more into mine. What I can see is the tops of some tall trees, including Tom and Kristy's pin oak.

That's going to look incredible when autumn comes around.

2
TEENAGE ANGST

In the month we spent looking at houses before settling on this one, Lisa and I discovered the problem with moving too far away from a city: if you intend to use your education at all, there are almost no jobs. Some jaded urbanite already had your idea and took the position you would have wanted.

Then we faced the problem with moving to the suburbs: if you're from there, like we are, it's the place you spent your teenage years trying to leave. Lisa and I felt a little defeated looking at homes in our old school districts.

Our real estate agent promised us something special when she took us to a house in Bloomsbury County, only fifteen minutes away from the neighborhoods each of us grew up in. The special thing was a driveway that could easily fit four cars, with a basketball net at the end of it.

The agent asked, Can't you just see playing ball with your kids here in a few years?

Yeah, I said, OK.

Neither of us really played team sports, Lisa said.

I see, the agent said. Well, if you're looking to start a family, they might like it, and all the space in the living room.

Sure, Lisa said, let's look at that.

The house was like every other house. Three bedrooms, two and a half bathrooms, unfinished basement, and a pretty big living room in need of wallpaper from the last quarter century.

The back yard, though, was walled off. Not with stones, with the spruce trees. I couldn't see over or between any of them except to glimpse the roofs and chimneys of my neighbors, and the Harrisons' pin oak. And we heard nothing, not a car or a lawnmower or a child.

Calm neighborhood, the agent said as we all stood on the patio.

Norway spruces, I said.

Excuse me?

Shhhhhh.

Lisa gave me an annoyed look.

Sorry, I said, but this is quiet, almost like when I went camping as a kid.

The agent forced out a laugh and said, We're not that far out.

No, I said, we're alone.

This yard is quite secluded.

It is, I said.

We walked out to the car parked in the driveway and saw the couple next door with their kid. She had green highlights in her hair, and wore ripped jeans and a pair of Doc Martens that may as well have been the ones Lisa still had in the back of our closet.

We spent the next few days talking about how, if we moved, we'd never find a cafe as good as the one by our apartment. We looked up the best restaurants in that area, and found that all of them were in strip malls. We wondered whether the cats would rather curl up next to the baseboard heaters in the house than on the couch with us.

But we woke up the next few mornings thinking about

that house, the back yard, the calm we felt there, how something about it was like home even without furniture or appliances.

We put in an offer and and had it accepted within a week of seeing the place.

Since we moved, I've gotten into the habit of taking a cup of green tea out to the patio after work. There's a half hour or so every afternoon when I'm the only one home because Lisa has a longer commute from her job in the city as St. George University's registration coordinator. I get to lean back in one of the white plastic chairs and keep both my hands around the mug while I listen to the breeze through our spruces, the birds flittering around. I can hear the few cars that drive by, or sometimes one of our neighbors throwing the door closed behind them after they come home from work, but that's it. It's always just me, my steaming cup, and my yard.

Now it's autumn, jeans and a hoodie weather.

Lisa has class tonight—as a school staff member, she gets to take one for free every semester—so I have longer than usual by myself before dinner. When I get home the sun's already sunk below the tree tops, and my lawn is wholly in the shade except for a few patches where the light pokes through the branches and needles, leaving bright spots like paint drops on the grass. Every sip of the tea makes a warm little trail down my chest which disappears in my stomach.

Perfect. I am alone in the universe. You wish you had an hour like this even once a month.

Then, my neighbor shows up.

Nathan! he shouts. Nathan, I'm glad I found you!

He must have already rung the doorbell and decided it was all right to tramp into my back yard when I didn't answer.

I put my mug down on the table and stand up to shake Alan's hand. He's shorter than me, too, but as thin as I am. Maybe thinner. His shoulder blades are so sharp they almost crease his shirt like a wire hanger.

Hi Alan, I say as I put my mug down on the table. What's up?

Sorry to bother you, he says, but are you and Lisa home tonight?

Um, why?

Our babysitter cancelled, he tells me, and we really can't get out of this dinner party. It's a big thing for my company. Can you watch Rayanne for us until we get back?

Wait, I say, you're only going to dinner?

Rayanne is fourteen. She's the girl we saw when we first looked at the house. I haven't actually seen her again, and I've only spoken with Alan a few times, mostly as we take our trash cans to the curb on Thursday mornings. Never long enough to warrant being invited into his house or meeting his family.

We should be home by eleven, Alan says. Maybe you could just have her over here to eat with you guys, then make sure she does her homework and doesn't watch too much TV?

I wonder why he didn't ask Tom and Kristy Harrison. If someone was going to put money on the next couple in this neighborhood having a kid, it'd be on them. The only conversation Lisa and I have had about kids is that we'll talk about it sooner or later. We don't even really like visitors our own age. Somehow, I guess, Alan sees competence in us. At least for a few hours.

Lisa calls me once her class ends.

We're having a visitor tonight, I say.

What?

I tell her about Rayanne, and that she'd better buy food for three of us.

Can't a teenager order herself a pizza or something? she says.

Guess not.

All right, I'll get stuff for a casserole.

Can you make it the Mexican chicken one?

Sure, she says. I hope that's what kids like.

Me too, I say. Alan's going to bring her over at quarter to seven.

Lisa tells me she'll be home before then.

I have to take mail, books, and empty shopping bags off the kitchen table since Lisa and I usually eat in the living room while we watch Jeopardy. Our cats immediately claim the new clean surface as their own and lay down like they're sunning themselves under the hanging lights.

Rayanne hardly speaks at the table. She whispers thank you when Lisa hands her a plate of casserole with avocado and sour cream on top. She eats slowly, in half forkfuls, and always finishes chewing before she answers our questions.

You're at North Bridge High School?

Yeah.

Ninth grade?

Yeah.

Do you like it?

It's fine.

In any clubs or anything?

Nope.

Spend a meal with a teenager when you're thirty two, and

you realize that fifteen years ago all the ways you thought you were different—all the energy you put into being more pissed off than anyone else—just made you more the typical kid.

You might see Rayanne as another disaffected teen, like we were, with her short answers and melancholy gaze at the floor. You might think of her as apathetic because of her ripped jeans, faded t-shirt, and dirty Chuck Taylors. But she also puts her napkin on her lap. She doesn't eat a thing until all three of us have full plates. She keeps her elbows off the table.

She's every teenager I've ever met except she has some refinement, which amazes me given the way her father ran into my back yard a few hours ago and shoved his daughter on us.

After dinner Rayanne asks to use the bathroom, and we tell her to use the nicer one upstairs.

That was painless, Lisa says as she brings the plates up to the sink for me to rinse off and put in the dishwasher.

Yeah, I say, maybe we'd be good parents.

If the kid was just like us, she says, but I don't think it works that way.

Probably not.

Then I drop a bowl in the sink and splash water all over myself.

Shit. I'm about as good a scullery maid as I would be a dad.

After I fill the dishwasher and start it running I go upstairs to change my sweatshirt. The door to the bathroom's open and the light's off. I figure Rayanne must have gone downstairs, but before I go into my bedroom I hear someone rustling around in there. I nudge the door open and see her by the dresser, looking at Lisa's iPod.

What the fuck are you doing? I ask from the doorway. Probably shouldn't have sworn, but I'm not used to this sort of thing.

Oh, she says. She's startled, and fumbles with the iPod.

What are you doing with that?

Nothing, she says. I wasn't going to steal it, if that's what you're asking. I mean, this is a fifth generation and I have a seventh. I couldn't sell this for ten dollars.

Then what were you doing? I ask.

Just looking through it, she says. You have a ton of Green Day.

That's my wife's.

Well, Rayanne says, she has some cool bands, but she's missing the good albums. Like with Green Day, American Idiot's not even on here.

I tell her that we don't recognize anything Green Day's done since we graduated high school.

She asks when that was.

1997, I tell her.

No way, she says, I was born in 1997.

I think, Fucking hell.

Rayanne, why are you here?

Are you talking, like, in the meaning of life way?

Why did your parents send you to dinner with us if they're going to be home in a few hours?

Because I'm a fuck up, she says. What, you think I can't microwave a burrito by myself?

Right, I say.

A few weeks ago my dad caught me going to a show at the Trocadero. I told him I was going to a friend's house to study, but he saw one of my text messages and figured it out. I didn't want to drink or anything, I don't even have a fake ID, I just wanted to see Band of Skulls.

I feel like a good father figure would go on to say something reassuring, something that would have a lasting effect. I keep listening.

I mean, she says, I know my parents did the same sorts of things I do that piss them off.

Everyone did those things, I say. Or they're Mormon, one or the other.

Yeah, she says.

You know, I was thinking about how much you're like Lisa and I used to be. There's one big difference, though.

What's that?

We never got caught.

I know Alan told me to make sure Rayanne does her homework, but Lisa and I kind of like the little punk—we want to hang out with her. I did make Rayanne apologize to Lisa for going through her iPod. After that, though, the three of us flip though the channels, find nothing on, and get to chatting.

Lisa asks her what other bands she likes.

Tegan and Sara, Titus Andronicus, Rancid.

No way, Lisa says, Rancid was my first concert. My dad took me and watched from the balcony of the Electric Factory. As soon as the show started I got totally enveloped by the mosh pit and he didn't find me until it was over. He was horrified, didn't let me go to another concert for years.

My parents still haven't let me go to a concert I wanted, Rayanne says. They took me with them to see Elton John last year, but I didn't really care.

Yeah, this is the time to see some good shows, I say. We

haven't been to a concert in a long time. You just grow out of it after a while.

My parents will never let me go, Rayanne says. They won't take me either.

You'll find a way, I tell her.

Lisa gives me a look.

I mean, you know, your parents will come around eventually, I say.

My first parenting fail.

She doesn't do any homework and I don't feel at all bad about that.

We talk a little longer about music and then Rayanne asks why Lisa and I moved out here.

A few months ago, I say, at two o'clock in the morning some guy walked up and down our street shouting into a megaphone. He said: Ignore the man with the megaphone. Most of the people in my office thought I was hung over the next day.

That's hilarious, Rayanne says.

Not when it happens to you, I say.

Seems more exciting than the crickets here, she says.

I guess it is, Lisa says, but that sort of stuff wears on you after a while. One day Lawndale doesn't seem so bad.

Where? she asks.

Lisa and I look at each other. Of course Rayanne's never seen Daria, she wasn't even born when it premiered.

You'll love this show, Lisa says as she brings out her DVDs and puts the first Daria disc in. Half way through the first episode I go upstairs and let the two girls watch it together. I don't actually know why I do that, since I like that show a lot, but it seems right to leave them alone.

I turn on the TV in our bedroom and half watch a MythBusters rerun. The girls laugh downstairs.

Lisa comes up after a while and tells me Rayanne is asleep.

Should we wake her up? I ask. Alan definitely wants her to do work tonight.

I won't, Lisa says. She crashed like she hasn't slept in days.

I go downstairs with Lisa and see Rayanne curled up in the corner of our L couch, the light from the TV flickering on her. Teenagers never look that peaceful.

We let her sleep. Lisa watches more Daria until she falls asleep too, and I go back upstairs. I pull out my laptop with every intention of checking my work email, but instead I sample some of the new Green Day albums.

They suck.

Well, I think they suck until I listen to some of the more popular new bands, who really suck. Then I go clicking back to American Idiot.

It just isn't as good as what I listened to when I was in high school.

You fall into stereotypes when you get old, too. You just don't care that much when you realize it.

So I decide to make Rayanne a mix from Lisa and me, except that of course we don't have a tape deck or tapes anymore, and I haven't burned a CD in ages.

Instead I make a playlist on a thumb drive and think the whole time how impersonal it is.

I'm my parents complaining about their AOL email accounts in 1995.

Once I hear Alan's car pull into the driveway, I have some Social D, Mudhoney, Screaming Trees, Jane's Addiction, and live Nirvana tracks on there.

That'll do for now.

I pull the flash drive out of the side of my laptop, then go down to the living room to wake up Rayanne and find both her and Lisa sleeping on the couch. Their heads are nearly touching in the corner of the L. Lisa fits on one side of the couch. She's small and curved, like a gymnast—her hips, her legs, her toes, even her face is rounded. Her short auburn hair, which she styles a little tousled, is smashed against one of the cushions. She has full lips, but when she's sleeping like this they get pouty, which kills me every time.

Rayanne's feet stick out over the end of the couch. She's taller than Lisa, but not lean, and her skin is much paler. Lisa looks like she has Mediterranean ancestry, though she doesn't, and Rayanne looks like she's from generations of English heritage. She does have the same round face. Her green hair covers half of it like a mask that's falling off, and as I lean in towards her I see that her skin is almost perfect, just one small blemish under her chin.

I shake her shoulder.

Your dad just got home, I say.

All right, she says, then rolls off the couch and walks toward the kitchen to grab her backpack just as Alan knocks.

Hey, I say.

She stops. I hold out the flash drive and tell her I put some music on it for her. She takes it, and puts it in her pocket.

OK, she says.

I don't know, I say, you might like it. It's some of my favorite stuff.

Cool, she says. Then she runs to get her bag.

I open the door and Alan shakes my hand, then asks if there was any trouble.

Nope, I say.

He looks around me and sees Rayanne with her bag slung over one shoulder.

Hey kiddo, he says.

Hi dad.

Run home and get ready for bed, he tells her, you've got school in the morning.

Rayanne shoulders her way past us and onto the front lawn.

She can be a handful, Alan says. She's rebellious.

Yeah, you know, she's a teenager, I say. That's what they do.

She's already done her fair share, he says, and we're really just at the beginning of it all.

It's funny, I say, Lisa and I think that any kid we have will rebel by being a cheerleader or a quarterback.

Alan narrows his eyes. He starts flipping his keys around his index finger.

I need to get better at dealing with awkward silences, or preventing them.

Listen, I say, I'm sorry, but she didn't do any homework. She fell asleep right after dinner and, well, we didn't want to wake her up.

Probably up all last night on the computer, he says.

Sure, I say. Anyway, like I told you, it was no trouble, we like her.

OK, he says.

After Alan leaves I sit on the couch with my laptop and look up some of those bands Rayanne mentioned earlier.

The thirty second samples wake up Lisa.

She says, Pick something to play already.

I'm browsing, I say.

She comes over and sits next to me, rubs her eyes and looks at the bands on iTunes as I click through.

I've never heard of any of these groups, she says. They're the ones Rayanne likes?

Yeah, I say, and I'd never heard them before either. But I like some of them.

Look at you, she says, liking new things. And new people.

What's that supposed to mean?

It's just not how you are, she says, new isn't really your thing.

Then she gets a little closer and puts her hand on top of mine. She says, Do you think we could put up with all of this?

What do you mean?

Every day, for five years or so. Bands we don't like, TV and movies we don't get, whatever clothes are in.

Maybe, I say.

And I think back to how my mother hated Pixies, how she almost didn't believe I could like music like that, and how my friends who introduced me to all my favorite bands worried her. I remember the way those songs were exactly what I wanted to hear even though I didn't know it until the first time Dan played Debaser for me in his car one afternoon, and how after he did I spent years trying to get a copy of everything like it. And how so very little else mattered.

Sure, I say, we could do it.

I think so, too.

3
THE IVY LEAGUE AND THE GUTTER

For years I didn't realize my cousin Reuben was such a shit, but if he wasn't I don't know if I would have met Dan, or when I would have heard Pixies for the first time.

Reuben's three years older than me. When I was five he told me that the tradition in elementary school was to lock the first graders in the mop closet over the weekend. Sometimes, he said, if the janitors were sick on Monday, no one found the kids until Tuesday or Wednesday. I remember him laughing while I ran upstairs to my parents.

When we got a little older and our parents would take us to Six Flags or a Phillies game, he'd push me while we walked so I'd run into a person going the other direction, or hit the bottom of my soda bottle just before I took a sip.

Because I was young, and clearly gullible, I thought he was cool, doing the things guys do to other guys.

By high school I knew he was just a moron who wore his Starter Chicago Bulls hat backwards, oversized t-shirts, and white high tops. But he did have a car. A loaded GMC Jimmy, actually. Which meant he was a moron with some friends and a girlfriend, even if the friends were idiots and the girlfriend had blotchy, oily skin.

He was a senior when I was a freshman, and though we wanted nothing to do with each other, his parents made him pick me up every morning on his way to school and take me home each afternoon.

It's a family thing, they said.

Despite the fact that his enclosed subwoofer sent vibrations through my colon on every trip, it was better than the bus.

On one of the first cold days in November, though, he left me at school. He didn't just leave before I came out of the building, he and his friends sat in the car and pulled out of his parking spot when I was about thirty yards away. They didn't do anything special, didn't yell at me or throw something towards me, they just laughed as they drove away. I still don't see why that was so funny.

I stood there for a moment, on the sidewalk outside the school, and watched them drive off, then thought about the best route home, whose yard I could cut through, if there was a Wawa along the way so I could get a drink. It was a six-mile walk back to my house, which was doable but a pain in the ass.

Then the car parked in front of me honked. The guy in the driver's seat rolled down his window and stuck his head out.

Hey, he said, don't you usually get a ride home with Reuben Jakob?

Yeah, I said.

I just saw him drive off.

I know, me too.

That guy's a piece of shit, man, why do you hang out with him?

He's my cousin.

So?

It's him or the bus, I guess.

That makes sense, he said. You want a ride?

Yeah, thanks, if it's not too much trouble.

I don't have shit to do.

When I got in the passenger seat the guy turned to me and put his hand out.

Dan, he said.

Nathan, I said.

This car, it was the worst car I've ever been in. A light blue Oldsmobile from the '70s with maroon interior, an analogue radio dial with cracked plastic, and an odometer reading 60,000 some miles. Dan would later tell me that it had already gotten to 100,000 twice and rotated back to all zeroes.

He pulled out onto the road and said, So, what's your deal, man?

My deal? I said.

Yeah.

Um, I don't really have a deal.

No? he said. Just an empty freshman?

I guess so.

At that point the only thing filling me up was my parents' expectation that I finish high school and go to college—a mirage four years away, which no one could clarify except to say that it was essential I get there.

So I asked, What's your deal?

Nothing special, Dan said. Trying to finish up here and then see what happens.

You're a senior?

Yeah. That's how I know your cousin's a fucker. I've seen that kid every day at school for years. Won't miss him after graduation.

Dan reached over and opened the glove compartment to

grab a tape which he shoved into the deck. I heard the clicking as the gears caught the spools, and the soft fuzz sound before the music came on.

Turn left here, I said, and go down Highland Street for a mile or two.

Then the music came on, the bass chords at the beginning of Debaser followed by the electric guitar hook.

Who is this?

Pixies, he said.

They're good, I said.

What do you usually listen to?

Not much, I said, I only have a few tapes people have bought me for birthdays and holidays. Nothing I liked. My parents listen to a lot of music, but classic rock, The Beatles and stuff.

This is a little better, he said.

Yeah it is.

Two songs later we pulled into my driveway.

Thanks for the ride, I said. And this band, they're The Pixies, right?

Just Pixies, Dan said.

Cool.

Then he popped the tape out of the player and gave it to me.

Here, he said, make a copy and give it back to me tomorrow.

Really?

Yeah. I mean, don't fuck it up or anything, I love that album, but it's cool if you make a copy tonight.

Thanks, Dan.

Sure, he said. Meet at my parking spot again after school.

Yeah, I said, yeah, of course.

Phat, see you then.

We had a boombox with two tape decks in the basement which my mom had bought but never used, so I hauled it upstairs, took one of those gifts which I'd listened to once and never again—We Can't Dance by Genesis—and taped Doolittle over it. Then I grabbed some masking tape, put a strip on both sides of the cassette, and wrote PIXIES on each one.

I listened to it three times that night while I did my homework. My mom knocked on my door after dinner and asked what it was.

Pixies, I said.

Oh, she said. She looked confused.

That's the name of the band, Mom. Pixies.

OK, she said. You like this?

I think it's really good, yeah.

Well, whatever you like. And is that my radio?

It was in the basement, is it OK if I use it?

Of course, she said. Then she left. For years she couldn't remember the name Pixies, and always called them Sprites, or Faeries, or even once The Little People.

After school the next day I met Dan at his car and a few other people were there with him. Reuben waited for me, but looked surprised when I walked to Dan's car instead of his.

Hey Nate, Dan said. This is Jon and Adelle.

Once I started talking to Dan, my cousin drove off, clearly feeling relieved of his duty. I actually haven't gotten in a car with him since then.

Jon looked like a smaller, thinner version of Dan: same baggy jeans, unkempt hair, and loose plaid shirt. Adelle wore the same kind of clothes as the guys, but tighter. She had her arms around Dan's waist.

I thought, Everyone calls me Nathan, I much prefer that.

But all I said was, Hey.

We're going to go to Houlihan's for lunch, Dan said, you want to come?

OK, I said, but I don't have that much money on me.

They all looked at each other and shrugged.

It's fine, Dan said, we'll get you today.

Thanks, man.

I reached into my backpack, pulled out the tape, and gave it back to him.

Wow, Jon said, you parted with that?

For a night, Dan said.

He plays that album all the time, Jon told me, I think he forgets they have four others.

It's the best one, Dan said.

I remember getting into the car and thinking how cool it was that I would get to listen to four more Pixies albums for the first time.

At Houlihan's we sat in the corner under some reproduced and over stylized posters promoting old boxing matches: Dempsey-Brennan and Marciano-Lowry. John ordered a plate of nachos for the table.

The three of them talked about some people I'd never heard of, probably seniors, but then realized I was sitting there quietly, taking a chip here and there, and started asking me questions.

What do you like to do?

I don't know. Nothing special.

What movies do you watch?

I don't go to the movies too often.

How's school going for you?

Fine, I guess.

Well, Adelle asked, what did you think of Pixies?

I listened to that album like three times last night, I said. It's so good.

Dan and Jon traded grins.

All right, Jon said, looks like someone will take our place next year.

I asked what he meant.

This school, he said as he took a sip of his soda, has overachievers or flunkies and nothing else. Talk to people, they'll all either say that they want to change the world or snort some Ritalin. Or both.

It's the Ivy League or the gutter, Dan said. Your cousin, by the way, is going to the fucking gutter. No one's... I don't know...

Genuine? I said.

Yeah, Dan said, that's it.

Bunch of posers, Jon said.

The waitress came over and filled our soda glasses, then asked if we wanted anything else to eat. We didn't.

You're not a moron just because you don't want to be a doctor or a lawyer, Adelle said. Or straight edge because you don't take every drug out there.

Do you guys? I asked.

What?

Get stoned?

They all laughed a little.

Fuck yeah, Jon said. Just, not all day, you know?

Sure.

Of course I didn't know. I'd never seen a joint before, and I knew kids who took Ritalin, but I'd never heard of anyone snorting it. I also knew kids who wanted to go to Harvard, but I didn't think much of it.

We spent the rest of the afternoon there, complaining about our school and drinking free refills on our sodas. They told me about kids who had anxiety attacks in the hallways before math tests, and others who got caught stashing weed in their lockers.

I thought they were exaggerating until I saw a girl hyperventilate later that year at the beginning of our Algebra mid-term. The proctor had to call the nurse's office and, while we waited for someone to show up, he dumped out a student's lunch bag so he could put it over the girl's mouth. A few minutes later they got that girl out of the classroom, but no one cleaned up the spilled yogurt from the lunch. It smelled like strawberries through the rest of the exam.

That girl ended up going to Princeton.

On the way out to the car after we'd finished eating, Adelle reached into her backpack and pulled out a tape.

Here, she said, copy this one tonight. Man cannot live by Pixies alone.

She gave me her Mudhoney album, which I copied over another unwanted gift, a Bon Jovi tape.

That weekend I asked my mom to take me to the mall so I could buy blank tapes in bulk, which still ranks as one of the best investments of my life.

I spent the rest of that school year tagging along with Dan, Jon, and Adelle wherever they went, which usually wasn't much further than someone's house the next town over, or maybe South Street in the city. They took me to parties, movies, even a few bars where the bouncers didn't care how old we were as long as we had money for drinks.

But most of all I listened to their music. During that year each one of them let me take a backpack into their rooms and stuff it with their tapes and CDs, which I then took home and copied onto blank tapes as quickly as I could. Bad Religion, L7, Alice in Chains, Temple of the Dog… They thought it was kind of funny the way I got into it so fast, how serious I was about listening to every grunge and alternative album available, but they were always happy to lend whatever they had.

Dan worried my parents a little when he stopped by one night after dinner. He rang the front doorbell and my mother answered it.

Hello, she said, can I help you?

I'm here to see Nathan, he said.

Oh, she said.

I came downstairs to see who it was.

Hey Dan, I said, what are you doing here?

I was on my way home from the mall and I just bought a new Tad CD. I thought you might want to copy it.

Cool, I said, I can do that tonight and give it back to you tomorrow.

He told me he could wait around while I copied it. Then he looked at my mom and added, If that's cool.

Oh, right. Mom, this is Dan Roffman. I told you about him.

Of course, she said. Nice to meet you.

I grabbed a blank tape and we went upstairs to copy the album, which took about an hour. We talked while the CD played and the tape turned in the deck, about school and maybe going to see Pulp Fiction that weekend, and we noticed both my mom and my dad walking by my bedroom every few minutes. I wonder if they were more worried about Dan, who that night wore jeans so old the blue had almost completely faded from them, or the music, which must have seemed unrefined and nonsensical to two Crosby, Stills, Nash, & Young fans.

Once the album copied I gave Dan back his CD and said, Thanks, man.

Sure, he said. See you tomorrow?

Yeah.

And then he left.

My mom and dad caught me before I could walk back upstairs to my room.

Nathan, my dad said, you know we trust you, but is he the right kind of person for you to be spending time with?

What?

We think he might not be the best influence, my mom said.

Why?

He seems…apathetic.

He is, I said. So are his friends.

It's just, my dad said, we're so sure you have a bright future, and—

OK, I said, I get it. Look, are my grades good?

They were.

Have I been out late on weeknights?

I had not.

Have you ever woken up and wondered where I was?

They had never done so.

Have I ever been arrested?

Of course not.

Then there's no problem, is there?

They looked at each other and conceded that, no, there didn't seem to be a tangible problem in that case.

OK then. I like my friends and I don't think they're a bad influence.

My parents said again that they trusted me.

I said, Thanks.

The last time I saw Dan, John and Adelle was at a party over winter break the next year. It wasn't supposed to be the last time, we all figured there would be another night when they were home from college and I could get away. There wasn't, and we just lost touch. No big goodbye, no long night of reminiscence. These things happen.

When Lisa and I went to Pixies' reunion tour a few years ago I hoped I might see one of them there, but I didn't. The two of us stood in the crowd and bobbed our heads to the music. I scanned the audience for familiar faces, but found none. I saw people with crows feet visible even in the dim light, guys with thinning hair dangerously close to a comb over, even one or two couples who brought their middle school age kids—no one at concerts ever seemed so old when we were in high school.

4
EVEN EAGLE SCOUTS GET FIRED

The guy I have to fire today looks old—he's bald and the skin on his face has started to sag—but he'd never go a rock concert. He stands at attention all the time, and wears wool suits through the whole year. He doesn't swear, and has never cracked a joke that wouldn't be appropriate for a ten-year-old. I don't know what his musical tastes are, but I feel like he'd have a collection of Andrews Sisters albums.

Firing him is an integral part of my job at Toaner.

My position as office manager is not to be confused with any sort of executive. The real executives at corporate headquarters tell me what to tell the sales people, the accountants, the HR sub-directors, then I relay the message and make sure no one fucks anything up. When someone does fuck up I tell the relevant executive, Sir, so-and-so fucked up. Yes Sir, pretty badly, or, No Sir, it was only a moderate fuck up, and then the executives tell me how they want it fixed or who to fire.

This time, Jim Walford, my best salesman, fucked up.

I first applied for this job through one of those massive search sites full of resumes from recent graduates. When the old office manager called me for an interview I was happy enough, when Sirs the executives called me for a follow up interview I was surprised, and when they offered me the job the next day I was shocked. The Sir who I talked to said I was the only one they'd interviewed who could properly put together a complete sentence, which the Sirs appreciated. One of them said, If we have to hear about someone who fucked up we want the report to be lucid.

This is how I make use of my communications degree.

I started as the assistant manager. At first I ran the place while the actual manager sat in his office with the doors closed and the blinds drawn, doing nothing work related that I could figure out. He often took a two hour lunch, and when he came back he left a trail of whiskey vapors between the front door and his office. After a few years he took early retirement and the Sirs promoted me. They said they weren't going to hire another assistant, that they considered the position unnecessary. That was fine with me, one less person to manage.

I have my own office, and I get to decorate it with volumes of Dostoyevsky on my bookshelf, which people look at with feigned curiosity; framed LP covers of Belly and R.E.M. albums on my walls; and, on my desk, pictures of Lisa, Iris and Virginia in our new house.

I almost never have to wear a tie. I do keep one in my desk, Windsor knot tied, ready to slip over my head and under my collar in case one of the Sirs deigns to come by.

They almost never do.

They love me.

I deliver their messages, I don't mess with their strategies—essentially I let the people in my office do their jobs. And when they don't I fire them, but in a way that they thank me afterward. No one ever tells me, or the Sirs, to fuck off. No one ever files suit against us after we get rid of them. When Jim Walford is unemployed in a few hours he won't either. I'm told that this is a pretty special skill, but it seems like common sense to me.

Jim Walford is an Eagle Scout. I should probably say he was one, but that's the sort of thing that sticks with people. He acts like an Eagle Scout.

Sometimes after we make a major sale a few of us go out for pitchers of beer. I won't miss Jim on those nights. He always kept his jacket on, didn't even loosen his tie. A few months after he started here he closed a huge deal, and I took him and everyone else involved to the bar on the company tab. We sat down at a high table with wobbly stools, placed our orders, and Jim saw me look a little longer than usual at our blond waitress as she walked away.

He asked me if I was married.

Yeah, I said, so what?

He was just saying…then his voice trailed off.

I wanted to tell him about the time Lisa and I were walking on the beach and she tripped while turning around to stare at some shirtless guy running past us. That was one of the best belly laughs we ever had, but I thought Jim wouldn't get it.

Clients love buying from Jim because of his Boy Scout ways, like how everything he says is proper, as if the conversation's being taped for future evaluation. He wears those wool suits every day, like a potential sale could walk in the door at any minute, even though our clients almost never see our offices, if they meet us in person at all. The internet can make business wonderfully impersonal. Still, on some Thursday afternoon when he doesn't even have a lead going, there he'll be, at his desk without so much as his tie loosened, while the rest of the sales team wears khakis and a polo, or even jeans.

He makes his coworkers a little uncomfortable, but he moves products.

I have to call Jim. I can see him out my office window. My office is in the back, so I can see everyone's desk if I leave my blinds open, which they are now. He's leaning back in his chair, on the phone, probably shoring up a deal with a client. I'll call him when I see him hang up.

Then my phone rings.

Hey, Mark says.

Shit, I say as I swivel my chair so I'm not facing the rest of the office. You're back.

Three months ago my friend Mark went to China, and he somehow turned it into an expedition through the mountains of Alaska. All I got from him after he left was a few point-of-fact emails: In China. Staying at a monastery, pretty cool. Met a guy who's taking me to Alaska. Going to climb Denali. I want to see him, to find out how exactly it all happened.

How are you?

A little jet-lagged, he says, and still cold, but I'm all right. When can we hang out?

I want to say, Right now, and take the afternoon off to see him. But there's Jim to take care of.

I ask, How's tonight?

This will be my reward.

Awesome, he says, there's this Chinese place in Jenkintown I want to try. It's legit dim sum, not American Chinese food.

Don't you want a steak or something, now that you're home?

Nope, I'm addicted to this stuff.

OK, I say. Do you mind driving?

Not at all.

Can you pick me up at 5:30?

Early, he says. We'll get a drink first?

Yeah, I say, I think I'll need it.

OK, see you then.

Now I have to call Jim. I could put it off until tomorrow, but even thinking that is strange. When the main office asks me to do something, I always do it right away.

I call Jim's desk, and watch him reach for his phone.

Hey Jim, I say.

Hi Nathan, he says, what can I do for you?

I need to talk to you this afternoon. Do you have some time around 5:00?

He says, I wanted to make Mitchell's soccer practice at six.

I think, Shit. Bringing up the kids...

Won't take long, I say. You'll make it, easy.

OK, he says, I'll see you in a few hours.

Great, I say.

When I hang up the phone, I get up and close the blinds, cut off the rest of the office.

I have an hour before Jim knocks on my door. I don't think he'll put up a fight, or even argue, since what he did cost everyone a lot of time, and the company a lot of money, but I don't want to do this one.

Not that what I want matters much. I got the final word from the Sirs this morning: Jim's got to go.

But Sirs, I said, it was a keystroke error, and could have happened to anyone, the part numbers for fiber optic links and optical A/B switches are only different by one digit.

They reminded me that it was my job to proof the big orders.

Lewis-Keane has ordered optical switches by the thousands before, I said.

So Walford fucked up, and not you?

That's right.

Well, we're getting rid of the one who fucked up on this scale.

I reminded them that Jim Walford was thirty five percent of our sales last quarter, that he beat out the next three sales people combined.

They told me I now have the opportunity to hire some new associates in that department to make up for it.

I said I understood.

Now I can't tell if I'm dreading this because I'll have to find a way to keep up the sales in the office, or because I suddenly care about him now that I have to let him go— fucking soccer game. I don't like firing someone, but it never makes me tense up in my core like it is right now.

I call Lisa.

Hey hun, I say, I'm not going to be home for dinner tonight. Mark's back, we're going to meet for dinner.

Finally, she says, he's all right?

Yeah, he didn't say he wasn't.

Did he go somewhere else after Alaska?

I think he came home from there.

Crazy trip, she says. Well, tell him I say hi. Bring back stories.

No problem, I say. How's your day going?

Fine. How's yours?

I have to fire Jim Walford today.

That guy did something wrong? she says.

Almost seven figures worth of something wrong, I say.

He stole?

No, I say, he messed up an order. A huge order.

Wow, she says. Well, I won't miss him at the holiday party this year. He creeps me out.

Yeah, I say.

You OK? she asks.

No, I say. I don't want to get rid of him.

You know it's not your call, Lisa says. You have strict bosses, what can you do?

I know.

Have a good time with Mark tonight, she says, whatever happens with Jim isn't your fault.

Thanks, babe.

Jim Walford knocks and I tell him to come in and have a seat. He has an American flag pin on the lapel of his blazer.

Before anything else he asks me how Lisa and I are settling into the new house.

Pretty well, I say. There are still a lot of boxes around, but it's livable.

That's great, he says, congratulations again.

He goes on to tell me that he solved the problem with Lewis-Keane, that they got the parts they wanted this morning, which was when we said they'd have them. The wrong order was rerouted to our warehouse before it got to their facilities.

I tell him that's good to hear, even though I already know all that.

But, I go on, we still have thousands of leftover optical A/B switches which will most likely be obsolete before we can sell all of them.

I see, he says.

You know how much that inventory's worth, I say.

Yes, he says, quite a lot.

It's a lot for us to have to sit on.

It is.

I have to be consistent with company policy, I say, which means that I have to let you go.

I understand, he says.

Jim didn't shake at all. Most people, when I fire them, you can see it click in their brains, and then wriggle down their spine. Not with Jim Walford.

Be prepared.

Listen, I say, this sucks. You've been one of the best salesmen in this office for the last few years, and now you're gone for basically a typo.

A typo worth hundreds of thousands of dollars, he says.

Sure, I answer, but still, a typo. You don't need me to tell you how pissed the execs are about this, but I'm not one of them. Keep this quiet, all right, but I'll write you a letter of recommendation to any company in the area. You'll have a new job soon.

He says, I very much appreciate that.

Well, it's no problem.

The Sirs, they know my shtick about the recommendation letter. They like it when I do things like that.

Thank you for being so considerate through this, he tells me.

He stands up, then wishes me the best of luck. We shake hands, trade finely honed grips.

And Jim Walford walks out. Job well done.

Hold on, I say. Jim, this sucks.

He looks at me but says nothing.

Jim, I say, this is crap. Don't you think it's fucked up?

I want to see the expression he gave me when he saw me checking out that waitress, but he doesn't show me anything close to that.

I say, Jim, c'mon, man.

I think I see him nod a little. Then he leaves.

I log off my computer and watch as whoever else is left in the office logs off theirs, kills the lights in their cubicles, and walks out the door into the parking lot. I'm the last one in the office. I'm usually the last one.

From my chair I see Mark pull up in his Land Rover, so I switch off my lights, set the security alarm, and lock the door. Mark jumps out of the car when he sees me, runs up and gives me a hug.

Welcome back, I say.

Good to be back at sea level, he says. You look like something's wrong.

I had to fire a guy today.

Did he deserve it?

Cost the company almost a million bucks with one typo.

Sounds to me like he deserved it.

Enough of that crap, I say, let's go.

We get in the car.

I ask, What's with this China-then-Alaska thing?

I had some wild times, he says, reminded me of when we used to cut Friday classes and drive into the woods for the weekend.

Yeah?

Yeah.

Mark puts the car in gear.

5
DISHONORABLY DISCHARGED

I met Mark the week before we started our freshman year at
Montcrief College. Some colleges offer retreats before the
term starts as a way for new students to bond, or to get a free
trip somewhere. Our school had a few: one to Washington
D.C., another to the beach in New Jersey—Mark and I both
signed up to go to to the Catskills.

I hadn't been camping in years.

My cousins always played football. After family dinners, while
the parents stayed at the table talking about those adult things
so mysterious to us at the time, the kids would go out back and
get into a game.

I never enjoyed that. Maybe it's because each time Reuben
would try to lay me out, but it probably had more to do with
the fact that I couldn't catch the ball in the first place. At that
age, there's not much else to the game.

One time my dad came out to see how we were doing
and found me sitting under a tree, watching everyone else play.
He asked why I wasn't playing.

I like it here.

Under this tree?

Uh huh.

Why?

I don't know, I said, I just do.

It is difficult to articulate the idea of inner peace at ten years old.

This was on a spring night, when the sun had set and the fireflies were out, but enough of a leaden blue light hung around for us to still see the silhouette of the wobbly football as it rose and fell over the field. With a cup of green tea it would have been the same feeling I now get on my patio in the afternoons.

OK, my dad said, if you're happy.

That June, once school ended, my parents took me on my first camping trip, which I doubt was coincidence. They brought out their musty canvas rucksacks they said they'd used while hitching to various music festivals during college, then talked about getting close to nature and some other sixties nonsense that even then didn't make much sense to me.

We drove to the Poconos, and when we arrived my dad bought a small pamphlet at the general store with some information about the local plant and animal life. We hiked, swam underneath a small waterfall, looked for constellations, but what I liked most was the afternoon we spent under a tree eating the lunch we packed back at the campsite. At the end of the trip I told my parents that next summer I wanted to go to a site with more white ash trees than American beeches because they give better shade. They asked how I knew the difference, and I pulled out the pamphlet from my back pocket.

They loved that. They thought I'd had an epiphany, or something, and bought me field guides to Pennsylvania's wilderness so I could read up and help decide where to go the next year. They also found their old copy of Living on the Earth. I liked the guides, but not the hippie book. I never wanted some spiritual revelation about my relationship with Mother Earth.

What my parents didn't understand then, what they still don't get about me, is that I just like being alone a lot of the time.

So we spent the next few summers in the Poconos, the Catskills, Shenandoah. My reading under trees went from guides to adventures, but real ones about the extreme outdoors, especially the highest mountains. I read all about Mallory, Herzog, Hillary, and Messner—the conquerors of those peaks—and got through nearly the whole canon of mountaineering books in a few summers. My parents and I hiked some of the graceful slopes of the Appalachian Mountains, always up and back on the same day, but I imagined myself approaching a Himalayan summit at the end of a months-long expedition, pretended I was struggling to stand in the rarified atmosphere of my ultimate goal.

By the time I was in high school I lost interest in family camping vacations, and spent my summers working retail jobs to afford CDs. I was either at work or in my room listening to grunge music—not outside, but still alone. Later I got into novels by Jack Kerouac, J.D. Salinger, and especially Kurt Vonnegut. Any man who can write a bestseller which includes a felt-tip pen drawing of an asshole is, to me, a hero of modern society.

When I got to choose a college, my first idea was reminiscent of those camping trips: a school with huge manicured lawns and a towering maple which the founder had planted a century ago, or something like that. But when I went on tours of Penn State, Ohio State, and Connecticut the student guides ran into dozens of people they knew. "Oh, that's my fraternity brother," "That's a teammate of mine," "She lived in my suite sophomore year." When I toured city schools everyone went about their business and spent more energy weaving between other pedestrians than anything else.

I opted for what seemed like my kind of people over my kind of setting.

This is how I ended up at Montcrief, a small liberal arts school in the middle of Philadelphia, only a half-hour from home.

When I signed up for the Catskills trip before college started, I did not consider the reality of a group composed of incoming freshman on a bus for four hours. The dozens of times I got asked where I'm from, why I chose Montcrief, what's my major, why I picked it, did I play any sports…That made for a fun ride.

Then there were the things the school had planned once we got there. I'd envisioned hikes, campfires, possibly finding some like-minded classmates. I got trust falls, health and safety discussions, and one afternoon talking about the ways to infuse positive energy into dorm life—whatever that means.

By our second night the whole thing had frustrated me, so I skipped out on the movie—they showed Mission: Impossible—and took a walk away from the cabin, among the mountain ash and pin cherry trees. After a few minutes I heard something rustling and saw an orange ember. The guy smoking noticed me and let his cigarette fall.

Hey, he said.

Hi.

Thank Christ, he said. Then he bent down to get the cigarette.

What? I said.

I thought you were one of the faculty.

Nope, I said.

We shook hands and introduced ourselves.

You smoke? he asked.

No.

It's not a cigarette, he said.

Still no.

How do you plan on getting through the rest of the trip, then?

I don't know, I said, maybe sneak away and live off the land until the bus is ready to leave on Saturday.

I'm in, Mark said.

We spent the next few hours meandering through the woods around the cabin. When we talked we mostly complained about the other students on the trip.

What's with the hippie girl? Mark said. Don't most people bathe before getting on a bus full of people they've never met?

Have you noticed that she doesn't wear shoes?

I saw her barefoot in the cabin, he said.

No, I said, she doesn't wear shoes ever. I asked her, she said she even goes barefoot on the subway.

Fuck, he said, I've seen used needles on the Broad Street line.

I know, right? And what about that little goth girl? She's like five foot two and wears those shit-kicker boots.

With the buckles? he said.

Yeah.

Oh no, man, I think that's hot. I wouldn't want to talk to her, but she'd be a wild ride. The guy that leers at her, though, he's fucked up.

What guy?

He looks pretty normal, Mark said, dressed like a Gap mannequin, but all he does is stare at people. He's always walking behind a group, not really part of it, but looking at them. Never smiles, never talks. He looks like he'll be a child molester after graduation.

Welcome to college, I said.

The next day we convinced the faculty leaders to let the two of us out of whatever was on the schedule, some exercise about what to do when you're stranded on a desert island, and hike around the area by ourselves. Why they let us is beyond me. Going out into the woods on our own, we were a lawsuit waiting to happen, but they said they were happy to see that we'd gotten close and thought it would be a good bonding experience, two young men, out in nature together, like a Coleridge poem...

Liberal academia worked out in our favor.

We didn't talk too much for most of the hike. We had a lake in mind we thought we could get to by mid-day, and along the way we really only spoke to orient ourselves on the map. The quiet was nice after listening to professors and advisers prattle on about the four years ahead of us, and other kids asking about the four years we just had.

Mark and I made it to the lake easily and had a lunch of granola bars and peanut butter and jelly sandwiches on the shore.

Were you ever a Boy Scout? he asked.

Yeah, I said, for about a month. I got kicked out.

No shit, he said, me too. This lake got me thinking about it. I was at one of those two-week-long camps over the summer and we were across a lake from the Girl Scout camp.

So one night I snuck out, put all my clothes in a trash bag and tied it to my waist, then swam across to the girls' camp.

You swam across naked? I said.

Yeah. I got dressed right after I got out. That water was freezing.

I guess they caught you, I said.

Some old lady came to the door of the cabin like five minutes after I got there. Not even worth the ridicule I got from my parents.

What I did was kind of worth it, I said. I went out one morning to climb a mountain.

Really? Mark said. That doesn't seem like something you'd have to sneak off to do in the Boy Scouts.

There's no mountaineering merit badge, I said. You'd think there was, but no. I asked the scoutmaster and my patrol leader if I could go, or plan a day with a group, but they said I couldn't, that people came out to work on merit badges and other skills.

That's kind of fucked.

I know. The kid I shared a tent with that weekend, he was working on his nuclear science merit badge. How do they have that and not a mountaineering one?

Sounds about right for them, though.

Yeah, I said, well, one morning before anyone woke up I slipped out to climb Camelback Mountain, which wasn't too far from our camp. I got there by lunch time and got to the top in an hour. The place is a ski slope in the winter, so it was really just a glorified hike on an incline. Then I got lost on the way back. I didn't have a map or anything, I just walked toward the big mountain without thinking how hard it would be to find our speck of a campsite in the woods later on.

Be prepared, Mark said.

I never was a good Boy Scout, I told him. So, it was dusk, and getting really cold. My shirt was soaked with sweat, and I didn't have any food left, so I sat down in a clearing pretty close to where I though the campsite was and waited. An hour later I saw a few flashlights, called out, and sure enough it was some guys from my patrol on the hunt for me.

They must have been pissed, Mark said.

They told me I ruined their day. The scoutmaster I think wanted to beat the crap out of me, but he'd already called my parents who drove up and were waiting at the campsite.

Holy shit.

Yeah. That was an intense ride home.

It was worth it, though? Mark asked.

I think so. I had this thing for mountains when I was a kid. I read all these real life adventure books about the Himalayas, so climbing a small one by myself was kind of cool.

Nice, he said.

Yeah.

We survived the rest of the week, and once we got going at Montcrief Mark and I started taking weekend camping trips to get away from the things that annoyed us about dorm life—the instant messages from people in the room next door, the unwashed neohippies from wealthy Main Line families, the roommates who'd leave a sock on the doorknob while they tried to sleep with very drunk girls. We'd blow off Friday classes and drive his 1983 Volvo up to French Creek or Hickory Run, find a place by a river, put up the tent and stay there until Sunday afternoon.

Cold, bad weather, none of that bothered us. If we felt

like getting off campus and out of the city, which we felt like doing pretty often, we'd go.

Mark and I had, and still have, a relationship with Philadelphia typical to many natives: we hate the place and all its provincial ways, all its idiots in Eagles jerseys who drink glasses of wudder or arange juice, but we won't move away. Even years later, when Lisa and I would get frustrated enough to leave the urban jungle, we bought a house less than an hour's drive from Center City. Mark travels the world now, but the address on his passport is still on the Main Line.

For the first two years of college, camping was our way of dealing with Philly, and it worked.

Junior year, though, I met Lisa, and Mark began work on his computer engineering thesis which would eventually make him rich. We still saw each other all the time, but the camping trips stopped.

After graduation, when most of our class went to Europe and stayed in hostels dirtier than our freshman year dorms, Mark and I had time for another trip and went hiking through the New England section of the Appalachian Trail. It was, we thought, the right way to end college.

We started in the White Mountains of New Hampshire and over the next few weeks hiked all the way to the end of the trail at Mount Katahdin. Like our first hike together in the Catskills, we were quiet through most of the days. It's amazing that we'd been hanging out all the time for four years and then, with weeks alone and no TV or movies, we said so little. And we were happy. The wood popping in the campfires and crunch of our boots over the rocks was enough for us.

On our last day, while we walked up the knife edge of Katahdin, I suddenly got chatty.

Did you know, I said, that the word excel means elevated?

No, he said, it doesn't.

Etymologically, I said. It comes from the Latin word *excelsus*, which means elevated or high.

OK, he said.

We were pushing up a ridge to the top of the highest mountain in Maine and this is what I wanted to talk about.

Superior, I said, was originally a Latin word meaning higher in situation. And sublime meant distinguished or raised above.

Mark said, Is this what you learned in your communications classes?

Some of it, I said. Some of it I looked up.

Who cares?

I do.

He said, Have you ever thought that you read too much?

Actually, yes, I have.

I didn't say anything else until we reached the rocky peak of Mount Katahdin and sat down to take in the view from the end of the Appalachian Trail. We looked over the green hills and valleys, the spots of little lakes that make up the Maine wilderness.

I don't like endings, I said.

What?

I don't like endings. That's why I started talking about words and height and stuff back there. When things end I get a little anxious.

And that makes you think about word origins?

I'm that kind of person.

Why don't you like endings? he asked.

I don't really know, that's just the way my mind works.

What's not to like about this? he said. We just walked a few hundred miles through the backwoods of New England and now we're at the top of a mountain. I thought you loved all those mountaineering stories. Well, here you are.

Yeah, I said.

Besides, we still have to get down.

It seems a little strange, I said, climbing all the way up just to get down.

You want a souvenir? he asked. A t-shirt or something?

Fuck off, I said.

We both laughed.

I looked around a little more at the panorama which had nothing higher than us. And no one else was even coming up the ridge.

This is pretty cool, I said.

Yeah it is.

We lingered up there a little longer.

6
FOCUS

Mark and I are sitting in the dim sum restaurant in Jenkintown. Since he picked me up I get to drink, and I need a few after firing Jim Walford. I've put down half a bottle of lager without eating, and a gentle fog rises up behind my eyes and into my head.

We only have one dish so far, which I don't believe is actually food. It looks a little like pasta, but I know it's not. Imagine one of those tourniquets the nurse wraps around your arm before drawing blood—it's like that, but chopped up, steamed, and seasoned. Mark spears a piece with a single chopstick and pops it in his mouth.

It's tripe, he says.

I know.

He tells me it's ginger tripe, that you only taste the seasoning.

Seasoned intestines are still intestines.

He says it's the stomach.

That doesn't help.

You spent three weeks in Japan on your honeymoon, he says, this sort of food can't freak you out now.

Getting exposed to it doesn't mean I have to like it. Besides, I'm convinced half the food we got in Japan was a joke on Westerners. Abalone? Come on.

Plenty of people eat that here, Mark says.

Never seen it.

They catch it off the coast of California, people cook it at barbecues.

Really?

The world might be a little bigger than what you've seen, he says.

Mark eats another piece of tripe. I take another sip and wait for the chicken portions to come around.

Mark's been gone for five months. He went on a six week eco tour through southern China, which turned into much longer stay in the Yunnan province. You either have to be poor or rich to pull that sort of thing off. Mark's independently wealthy.

His money comes from an advancement he made in storing digital information, some way he found to make servers a hundred times more compact and efficient. He worked on this through college and presented it as his senior thesis. It actually took a few years after that for hardware technology to catch up with Mark's brain, but once it did he patented the thing and now he never has to worry about money again.

I don't understand exactly what he did, but he once told me I use it every day without even knowing it, every time I log onto my company's network.

Cool, I said.

As we grab more dim sum dishes and reorganize the table settings to fit them in, he tells me about how his Chinese trip began with a backpacking tour around Pudacuo National Park. He says that everyone carried with them all the things they'd need for days at a time, that he saw Himalayan yew trees which I would have thought were pretty cool, and how doctors have found some sort of cancer drug in their extract. Then he starts on about the Irish girl who basically gave him a course on Buddhist meditation during the hike, telling him the whole time how it was the ultimate tranquility.

After the tour she went to a Yunnan village to live in a monastery, and Mark followed her. They ended up staying there together for three months.

While there, Mark meditated every morning with the priests at the temple, people who couldn't even conceive of the things he'd invented and for whom there could be nothing more than their ancient rituals. The place was on a hillside, looked out over a lush valley, and Mark said he'd never been somewhere so quiet and focused. He liked that, for a little while, but started asking himself what he was focused on. He never found an answer.

So when Sig, a New Zealander who'd just finished climbing some mountains in the Dequin district, met a disillusioned Mark in the village, it wasn't hard to convince him to leave. Sig was on his way to Kunming to get a flight to Alaska, where he planned to climb Denali. He offered to let Mark come with him and try an ascent.

So this guy you met in rural China, I say, he just offered to take you all the way to Alaska and let you tag along to the top of Mount McKinley?

I paid my own way, Mark says, and a fee to be a part of the expedition.

Did he know that you'd never climbed a mountain?

Sure. But he also knew about all the hiking and camping I'd done with you, our time out on the Appalachian Trail.

Shit, Mark, that's not like climbing a mountain.

No, he says, but it was enough for Sig. The guy's crazy, he goes from mountain to mountain without a break, says he hasn't been to his house in Auckland in two years. The whole time he kept saying "higher, up higher" in a voice that sounded like his throat was still frozen from his last high altitude trip. We got on a plane and he slapped me on the back, "higher, up higher." When we saw the Alaska Range he growled at me, "higher, mate, up higher." I swear he snored it.

He snored in words?

It just sounded like he did, Mark says.

And you went with him?

He's still alive, so he must be a pretty good climber.

Mark tells me that the climb was hard, though not as hard as he thought it would be. Life on the mountain got strange, but no one got close to losing appendages.

Sig took him to an outdoor shop in Anchorage and got him properly outfitted, then they went by bus to Talkeetna where the two other members of the expedition, both Kiwis, picked them up in a van that looked as if they should abandon it on the side of a highway and hitch to the mountain—for safety's sake.

The three New Zealanders had climbed together for years, knew each other since high school. As they drove, Sig told the other two about Mark, and they welcomed him with skepticism, but after a few days he earned a certain respect.

Essentially, he shut up and did what the other three told him to do. The guys he was with, they knew they were the experts, and they didn't want suggestions on how to hammer a piton or fasten a rope from someone on vacation. When they said to push on because they had to reach a camp by dark, he did.

When they said to slow down due to a crevasse they somehow sensed was under the snow ahead, he did. He carried what they told him to, handed them any equipment they asked for.

One night the winds seemed to cut through the tent, and it got dangerously cold, so they took off their boots and warmed their feet on each other's bellies. They didn't have to ask Mark, he saw them and knew it was what he had to do. This method, Mark tells me, is one of the best ways to prevent frostbite when you're on the side of a mountain, and that when you spend days on end with a group of guys and no shower, it's not even awkward.

He swears it was all liberating. Every morning he took five minutes to meditate and focus, but on Denali he actually had something to focus on, a goal.

He says that climbing was similar for his three partners, that it was an end for them and being there was all they wanted. They smiled the whole time, at the end of ten hour climbs and in the coldest wind as they approached the summit. When Sig growled "higher, up higher," they grinned at him. Mark says they would have laughed but it hurts at that altitude and in that cold.

I picture them the way I picture outlaws of the Old West laughing through gun fights.

When the group summited, everyone took pictures, but no one celebrated more than a crack of a smile or a pat on the back. They only stayed for twenty minutes or so.

They left like they had an appointment to keep with another mountain.

Mark says that he thought going down would be disappointing, but it was the same as the ascent: get up alive, get down alive. How you do it doesn't matter so much, just reach your goal of the next camp, the first town, then home. If you do, you're great, if you don't, you probably die.

Something to focus on.

So, I say, that explains things.

Explains what?

Why you never called, you never wrote.

Oh, Mark says, were you sitting in a dark room waiting for me to call?

Yeah, I say. Me and your bubby.

Italians don't have bubbies.

I've met your grandmother, I say, and even though she's from Sicily, she's your bubby. Trust me.

By this point we have almost a dozen half empty dim sum dishes, most of which are the appetizing parts of fowl, shrimp, and beef. Mark has a few filtering organs which I won't touch. And feet, I leave his order of chicken feet alone.

So, I say, who'd you run into on your way home to take you on the next adventure?

Actually, one of the New Zealanders.

Really? Where'd you go?

Nowhere yet, Mark says. We were on the mountain for three weeks, so from Anchorage we all went home except Sig, he went to the Canadian Rockies. But one of the other guys, Ray, he's the lead guide on an expedition next May, and I think I'm going to go.

Where to?

Mount Everest.

Bullshit.

No, it's for real. And I wanted to talk to you about that. You should come with me.

Wow, I say as I put an entire shrimp dumpling in my mouth. While I chew, Mark stares at me with that Wild West grin I pictured on his climbing partners—his lip pulled up just a little higher to one side, showing that he thinks he knows more than me.

You've been gone a while, I finally say, but I thought I told you that I bought a house a few months ago. Our spare bedroom is still storage for the boxes we haven't opened. So, I can't really take a lot of time off and haul to the Himalayas, what with my new mortgage. And I've got a wife who'd be pretty pissed if I died on the side of a rock. Oh, and I've never climbed a mountain.

What about Maine?

You really want to compare that to Nepal?

OK, he says, but you keep in shape out in the suburbs?

Sure, I say. I pass an LA Fitness and two Gold's Gyms on the way to work every day. You almost join one by accident at that point.

Well that's enough.

It is not enough, I say. I run on a treadmill like twice a week and maybe lift a few weights if Lisa's also there and she reminds me to. Yeah, you and I camped a lot, but the only time I've even seen a real mountain range is when I had a layover in Denver a few years ago.

People without much experience, and in worse shape than you, climb Everest every year, he says. The guides are there at every moment, they know how to get you to the top. We'll train together, it'll be a good time.

Mark, really. This isn't going to happen.

Fine, he says. He sits back in his chair and tells me he just wanted to offer, that he thought I'd really want to do it.

Of course I want to do it, I say, I've had daydreams about the Himalayas since I was a kid. It's just completely implausible.

We finish up the dim sum and sip on the remaining beer in our bottles. Mark asks if I want a little something extra after we're done.

Are you still smoking?

Of course, he says, you still don't?

Not since college.

But, he says, now I can afford good stuff. I've got basically a two hundred dollar joint in the car. Strictly mellows you out, none of that weed hangover you used to get.

No thanks, I say, but I could go for another beer.

Cool.

He flags down the waiter and orders another round. At this point every other table is getting to their fortune cookies and orange slices. I have a feeling we're going to close the dim sum place.

So, Mark says, does Lisa want to have kids now that you guys have a home and all?

We haven't really talked about it, I say.

At all?

Well, over the years, in the abstract, sure. And we actually babysat for our neighbor's daughter a few weeks ago.

That's great, he says, how did you and Lisa handle a toddler?

She's fourteen.

What?

I tell Mark about Rayanne, her dad coming into my back yard, the music, her being a bit of a screw-up.

You really like her, Mark says.

Yeah, she's cool.

Is she hot?

Fuck you.

I didn't ask if you were going to try and bang her.

Still, I say, that's messed up. She's an alt-kid.

Just like the girls you used to go for?

Just like I used to be. And Lisa liked her a lot, too.

But you're the one who gave her some music.

Yeah, I thought she was cool enough to give some MP3 files. Real inappropriate things going on there.

OK, Mark says, you're right, but that's still new. You've never loaned me a CD.

That's because you have shit taste in music. Why I hang out with a guy who owns so many Oasis albums is beyond me.

You know that there's more music on the planet than just what's on your iPod.

But most of it sucks, I say. Although, Rayanne told me about a few bands I'd never heard of that were all right.

Look at this, you're taking recommendations from a teenager. I can't tell if she's your minion or your buddy.

Just the cool kid next door, I say.

The waiter comes over and puts two bottles of beer on the table.

All right, Mark says as he picks his up, cheers to your new home and everything that comes with it.

Cheers, I say.

68 JOSHUA ISARD

7
MORNING COFFEE

I pull into the garage around midnight.

Lisa's waiting up for me when I walk inside. She's sitting on the couch with her legs folded under her, wearing jeans and a now wrinkled tank top. Her hair is matted down on one side. I can see a few of her toes poking out. They're little and chubby and freshly pained with dark polish.

Are you drunk? she asks.

No, I say. Are you?

A little, she says.

I'm standing just inside the door and she's twisted herself around to look back at me. A bottle of wine's on the table, and the glass next to it has a sip of red left. Neither of us move.

Why didn't you call me? she asks. Or text?

You knew I was out with Mark, I say, so there was nothing to tell you.

She says she didn't want an update, that I just could have said, Hi.

Were you worried about me? I ask.

Not really, she says, but a little contact would have been nice.

I haven't seen Mark in months, I say, I was a little caught up in it.

So, you forgot about your wife, she says.

No, I say.

Then I stop. Five years ago this would have been a smackdown over relationship theory. I would have asked why she didn't send me any texts if she wanted to hear from me so badly, why I couldn't just enjoy a night with my friend who I haven't seen in so long. But after a little while I figured out that there are some things my wife wants which I can't predict. If Lisa was out with her friend and sent me texts every half hour, I'd get a little annoyed and assume she was bored.

Sorry, hun, I say. I didn't realize how much that meant to you. My fault.

She doesn't say anything, though she does give me a look with wide eyes and slightly pursed lips that she wants to be evil, but which I know means she's already over it. Lisa's genuine evil looks are instinctive. And terrifying.

I sit down with her on the couch.

She asks where we were that we stayed so late.

We went to that dim sum restaurant, I say. Mark wanted to try it.

How was it?

I thought a lot of the food there was a joke.

It wasn't good?

It wasn't food.

She says that I need to embrace the fact that other cultures have different cuisines.

I remind her that I'm from Polish peasant stock and, therefore, have a strong aversion to unusual textures—and to flavors in general.

She sighs.

In Scotland I tried haggis and king rib. In Japan I tasted some neon blue thing, and neither of us could conclude whether it was once animal or plant life. When you travel, you do that sort of thing. In Bloomsbury County Pennsylvania—home to lousy Italian red sauce restaurants, a few hibachi places, and three Olive Gardens—I'm not looking for adventure.

So, she says, you guys closed the place?

Yeah, I say. It was a little strange doing that, but as long as we kept ordering, the staff was happy to have us there. They just cleaned around us.

OK, she says, what did you talk about?

Oh, I say, his trip. He had a good time.

That's it? she asks.

Well, I say, you know he went to China and Alaska.

Nathan, you were with Mark for five hours, and all you bring me is that he had a good time?

So I tell her about China, living in the temple, Sig and the New Zealand mountain climbers. I tell her about how Mark really found enlightenment on the side of Denali instead of in a temple custom built for just such a thing. And, I say, Mark asked me to come with him on the next trip.

She asks if he'll be gone for six months again, and how my bosses will like that.

Well, I say, about three months actually, but I can't do that either.

I know you can't, she says. Where's he going?

Nepal.

Three months in Nepal? she says.

It takes three months to climb Mount Everest.

Holy shit. He's going to do that?

Yeah, one of the guys he climbed Denali with is going to lead an expedition in May. Mark's on it.

And, she says, he wants you to do it with him? Does he

know that the closest you've been to a mountain are those books you read and an IMAX movie we saw a little while ago?

That's what I told him. He said that novices climb every year and that as long as I'm in shape I should be fine. We camped in college, and for a long time along the Appalachian Trail, so, you know, that part would be all right.

Have you been camping since then? she asks.

No.

So why on Earth does he think it'd be a good idea to take you to the Himalayas? I mean, he was pretty stupid climbing in Alaska, right?

Yeah.

So, this is even worse, she says, especially for you.

Look hun, I say, I'm not going, all right?

A few minutes later we're up in the bedroom, pulling the blankets over ourselves. Lisa clicks off her lamp, but I leave mine on. She tells me to just go to sleep, that I'm going to be miserable in the morning.

I know, I say.

It's at this point that I wonder if trying to go to sleep will only make things worse in the morning. I pick up my paperback copy of Morvern Callar and read a paragraph. Then I read the same paragraph again. The words don't seem to be sticking with me.

Lisa rolls over, clicks her light back on, then turns to me and asks how I'm not exhausted.

Just not, I say.

She sits up.

She says, You're never just not tired. You can fall asleep anywhere you want after about eleven.

Not tonight, I say.

Yeah, why?

I don't say anything. I know why I'm still awake, but I still think I can get away with the broke-my-routine or had-too-much-to-drink excuse.

Nathan, she says, use your words.

I want to go, I say. I want to go with Mark.

You're insane.

No doubt.

There's no way you can do that, she says. I'm not going to let you try.

I want to go, that doesn't mean I will.

She tells me that it definitely does not.

It just seems...special, I say. You know I've loved stories about mountain climbing since I was a kid, and I never really thought I'd ever have a chance to go.

Oh, she says, and going to Japan for three weeks wasn't special? Most people go to Hawaii for their honeymoon, they stay in a resort they don't have to leave. And what about our time in Britain, and that trip to Budapest we took last New Year's?

I tell her I know, that I love all that. But that's traveling, anyone with the time and the money can go. This is talent. Or skill. Something like that.

And you have that talent? she asks.

I don't know, I say.

I get out of bed and pour a glass of water in the bathroom. I ask Lisa if she wants one, but she says no. When I get back in bed she reaches over, grabs my glass, and takes a sip.

I thought you didn't want one, I say.

I don't, she says, I just want a sip of yours.

She smiles at me.

You know I love you, she says, and support you. I just don't want you to get killed doing something stupid.

I know.

She asks what makes me want to do this, anyway.

I tell her that I don't know exactly. Mark was talking about focus, how he could have something straight-forward that he needed to do, and do it. It's kind of like that. It's not easy, but it's simple. I can't make politicians tell the truth, I can't make it so Jim Walford keeps his job, I can't stop wars, and I can't make the average person intelligent. But if I try, maybe I can climb a mountain.

OK, she says. Well, maybe you don't want to start with the biggest one.

Yeah, maybe.

Lisa gets up first the next morning and makes me coffee. She never does that. It's one of those things—every morning, seven days a week, I get up, grind the beans and make the coffee. But this morning I wake up, the sun's sending streaks of light through the blinds, and our French press is on my nightstand.

Hun, I say.

I hear her come up stairs and back into the bedroom. She's only wearing a towel wrapped around her body. Her hair is darker for being wet, almost black, and leaves little droplets on her shoulders.

Morning, she says.

I sit up and swing my legs over the edge of the bed, then throw the duvet off to the side.

I say, Morning, babe, what's with this?

You had a long night, she says, so I thought I'd take care of things. I've got lunch made for both of us, I emptied the dishwasher, and I gave Iris and Virginia fresh water. I even wound your watch.

Wow, I say.

Something wrong? she asks.

Not at all, I tell her, except that I don't see my pouring the coffee straight into my mouth as a good plan.

Shit, she says.

She runs downstairs and brings up two mugs. The towel only covers the very top of her thighs, and not even that when she sits down next to me and crosses her legs. Her skin is tight around the curves in her legs and arms — they look hard and smooth, each like a stone taken from a riverbed.

I think about morning sex.

It's not late, I say and run my fingertips over her leg.

Oh, she says, you're not usually like this on a weekday morning.

Apparently this is a special morning.

You look good, she says while taking an exaggerated look up and down my body. Have you been going to the gym more than usual?

Nope, but I really should.

Then I run my hand up her back and through her wet hair. I want to pull her in for a kiss.

I say, Maybe instead we could get a workout now.

Lisa laughs. She says, Relax for a minute, cowboy, we don't have time for everything. But all you have to do is shower, get dressed, and go. I've got everything else.

I take my hand away and lean back on my elbows.

This is all right, I say, I should stay out with my friends every night.

It's not that, she says. I don't understand what you were

saying, about why you'd want to go, but I trust you. With those stacks of books you read, and the way you and Mark used to go to the woods in college—this must be something that means a lot to you.

Thanks, I say.

I give her a kiss on the forehead.

I still don't think you should go, she says, but I know you don't bring up something like that lightly. I mean, how often do you even have the opportunity?

Not often, I say. And then, we don't have the money. A trip like this costs about thirty grand.

Shit, she says.

Yeah.

Well, it's too dangerous even if it's free. You have responsibilities.

I say that I think my bosses would find someone to replace me after a few seconds of mourning.

What about me?

Not to downplay the tragedy of my death on Mt. Everest, I say, but you'll be fine, too.

That's not what I'm talking about, she says.

And I look at her.

I ask, Are you?

No, she says. But…

I tell her I thought we were going to talk about this before we made any decisions.

She says, We did. Remember listening to that music after Rayanne left?

That was not a conversation, I say, that was kicking around an idea for a few minutes.

It was a start.

So then, do you want to?

I'm thinking about it.

You're thinking you want one?

Yeah, she says, a little part of me does.

Is that enough?

I don't know, Nathan. We're not on the way to the delivery room, we're talking it over.

I think to myself about how this is a harsh concept to get hit with before I finish my first cup of coffee and when I thought I was going to get laid. We wouldn't be able to sit on the bed like this anymore, her in a towel, me in nothing. Not until we're fifty or so. I guess when your biological urge is to fuck rather than nurture you think about having children in negatives.

Last night, she says, when you mentioned going with Mark, I didn't think of becoming a widow, I thought of our child being half way to orphanhood.

Our child that doesn't exist, I say.

Right. I just want you to know what I thought about.

I put my mug down and give Lisa a hug. Sometimes, when I don't know what to say, that's the best option.

We'll talk more? I say.

Yeah, she says. Then she gets up, takes a few steps toward the bathroom, and undoes the towel, lets it fall down her back slowly. She turns her head back to me. When we get home tonight, she says, then you can run your hands anywhere you want.

Fuck, I say.

Not first, she says, there's plenty to do before that.

And I get a hard-on there on the bed which I can't entirely get rid of through the whole day at work.

8
JEREMY BENTHAM'S HEAD

Lisa and I don't take long in getting back to our routine—more discussion about pumpkin spice lattes coming back at Starbucks than about kids—when a serious Indian summer hits. It's gorgeous weather for early November, which has ruined our weekend. All the reports start telling the tri-state area that no one will need a coat for the next few days, and my parents promptly invite us over for dinner on Sunday night—last time eating outside until spring, they say. And we haven't been over there in a while.

And we never call, and we never write…

Then Alan Gillian invites us over to celebrate his birthday on Saturday evening. He says that his birthday party hasn't been outside since he was thirteen, that this would be just like if he was born in the springtime. He hadn't been planning to do much, but what with the weather he was going to invite every house on the street.

Before we could make plans, we couldn't.

As we get ready to go over to the Gillians', Lisa tells me that I have to tone it down for a party like this.

Tone down what?

Well, she says, you can't talk about the engagement ring, for one.

When we got engaged one of the questions people kept asking us was whether or not the diamond was ethical. I hadn't thought of that when I bought it. Like any good Jew, I know someone who has a friend in the jewelry business, a wholesaler actually, and he gave a me a great deal on the rock and the setting. That was the extent of my shopping.

We tried telling people that we didn't know exactly where it came from, but they said to find out. A few times we simply said that no, it isn't. We got some indignant looks. So we started saying that it isn't ethical, and that instead of the GIA certification which usually comes with a diamond we got a list of casualties associated with it—that way we know it's an authentic blood diamond.

You know who your friends are by who laughs at a joke like that. We don't have too many.

Lisa says, Don't talk about things like the Greenpeace guy outside Whole Foods.

She means the way I won't sign his petitions against greenhouse gases. No, she really means the way I tell him I'd rather not because if Philly's on the beach soon then my property value will skyrocket.

Lisa finishes putting on her make-up and I finally decide to go with a long sleeve shirt instead of a polo, then we leave. As we walk over I say, It's not just me. Remember Kim's baby?

Lisa thinks a moment and then says, Oh yeah.

We were out to dinner a few months ago and Kim, who we knew from college but hadn't spoken with since, was at the restaurant with her husband and baby. She came to our table and introduced us to Charlotte. Sometimes she's Charlie, Kim said, when she's feeling more casual. And sometimes she Lottie, when she's just too cute. She's got a nickname for every mood!

That's perfect, Lisa said, if she's transgendered she can be Chaz. You've got it all covered.

As we leave our house, Lisa tells me that she probably won't mention that.

As we walk over to the party, Lisa and I agree that we're going to try and stay together during this thing. We'd met most people on our block peripherally:

You're the new couple, right?

Yep.

We shake hands.

We agree to meet sometime soon.

Welcome.

Thanks.

But we'd only really gotten to know the Harrisons and the Gillians.

We go through the gate in their split rail fence and into their backyard, a big square one that slopes up away from the house, spotted with three white oaks and a swing set they need to take down. Alan takes good care of his yard, and I know this because I can hear him doing so every weekend—riding his lawnmower, using his motorized hedge trimmers. I can respect this since I also take care of my yard every weekend, but I use a battery powered mower. No noise, no fumes. I put on my iPod and I have my idyllic American-style hour of zen. And cut grass.

Ten people or so are already at the party. Some kids, elementary school age, run around the yard but I can't tell if they're playing a game or on a sugar rush. The Go-Go's Our Lips Are Sealed plays through the Gillians' cleverly concealed outdoor speakers. We grab at each other's hands when Alan and his wife, Nancy, see us walk through the fence gate.

Alan says hi to me, tells me he's glad we came, thanks me again for watching Rayanne, asks me what kind of beer I want, puts his arm around my shoulder and takes me over to the cooler next to the wood deck where the group of guys are standing.

Nancy says hi to Lisa, tells her what a lovely sweater she's wearing, thanks her again for watching Rayanne, asks if she'd like red or white, takes her arm and leads her over to the table on the deck with bottles and glasses around which the women are standing.

At the cooler Alan offers me a choice between microbrews I've never heard of and that mass produced stuff which resembles the urine of a small insect. I guess at one of the microbrews. It's hoppy and bitter, and pretty good.

I glance at Lisa, who's accepting a glass of red from Nancy, and see her stand up extra straight as she's introduced to a few other wives.

Nathan, Alan says, you've met these guys, right?

There are a few people I've talked to for a combined total of three minutes. Tom Harrison is also there, and he stands out for being so short. Everyone else is my height, within an inch or two. But except for Alan these guys are all big. Some are bulky like Tom, but a few are just fat, with shirts that fit so tightly around their bellies you'd think they were proud of them.

Yeah, I say, we've all talked before, but only for a minute.

We do the introductory occupation-college-family conversation for a while, and when I look over at Lisa I see her doing the same thing.

It takes an hour before everyone arrives and the genders start to commingle. Lisa and I end up sitting on folding chairs which wobble on the grass, talking to three people who live on our block and graduated from Drury University, Montcrief's rival. They can't help but tell us how much they disliked our college.

One of them says, We stole all the hockey pucks from Montcrief's training room the night before a game. It was hilarious watching them warm up by just skating in circles.

I was a bartender in Old City my senior year, another tells us, and anyone wearing a Montcrief shirt got served last.

Lisa and I laugh along with their stories. We never understood the animosity between schools—they were mostly engineers and we were liberal arts kids, so the two groups would never compete for anything. I think the feud only exists because students are told during freshman orientation they're a part of it.

But we can't stay silent, we'd look humorless.

So Lisa says, There was this crazy rivalry at the school I went to during my study abroad in England. Jeremy Bentham founded the university, and they keep his embalmed body on display in a hall of the main building. The students from across London used to sneak in, steal the corpse's head, and play soccer with it on the quad until someone caught them.

I'm glad she says something, but no one else is.

Only a few minutes later our neighbors excuse themselves to other conversations and Lisa and I sit on the chairs by ourselves.

This isn't so bad, I say.

They think we're freaks, she says.

I just want it on the record that you told that story, not me.

Lisa sighs.

They're going to think we're freaks anyway, I say. No one tells a story about Jeremy Bentham or his head at a garden party.

And no one calls it a garden party, she says. I mean,

I studied his philosophy across the hall from his body, in the school he created. No one else would think that's cool, would they?

Probably not on this block. Do you think anyone here knows who Jeremy Bentham was? They don't want to travel to London, the furthest anyone here's interested in going is their house at the shore.

Maybe we are just going to be the strange ones. I listened to a conversation about the best way to make sure your toddler doesn't get rejected from the preschool on Pinewood Avenue. Who rejects toddlers? They were all so matter-of-fact about it, like their three year olds were applying to college.

So we won't bond with our neighbors. Is that so bad?

Maybe. I would have liked to.

Me too, if they were cool. But I didn't expect them to be. Did you?

I don't know. I hoped.

I think that this isn't much different from when we lived in the city and saw hipsters in cafes pretending to read Finnegans Wake. We didn't try to get to know them either. This sort of thing doesn't bother me, I've accepted that the chances of connecting with someone new in a meaningful way are so small that it's not even worth trying. But I don't say that. Instead I just tell Lisa I have to use the bathroom.

You're going to leave me here? she says.

Unless you want to come with, I say.

She goes for more wine instead.

The Gillians' downstairs half bathroom has a dog theme. They have dog pictures on the walls of all different breeds from St. Bernards to Highland Terriers, bars of soap shaped like paws, and a ceramic dog in the corner which holds an extra roll of toilet paper in its mouth.

They don't own an actual dog. My cats are laughing from my house.

When I walk out I see Rayanne in the kitchen.

Hi, I say.

Hey, she says.

She's wearing a yellow t-shirt and cords, and they fit snugly around her chest and hips. As soon as I notice that I make sure to lock on to her eyes, which happen to be pretty and brown. Like Lisa's.

I say, What's with the dog thing in the bathroom?

My mom loves dogs, she says, but my dad's allergic. So we get that.

Oh, I say. I didn't even know you were here.

Yeah, just trying to avoid the herd.

It's your dad's birthday.

Looks like all his favorite people are here to celebrate it with him, she says.

Right.

I ask her what she thought of the music I gave her.

She says it was all right.

All right? I put songs by The Breeders on there, some Dinosaur Jr., Sleater-Kinney…

Yeah, she says, some of that was pretty good. I liked that Dig Me Out song.

It's off a great album, you'd like the whole thing. Look at the album art, too, it's a tribute to the Kinks.

I don't listen to them much.

I laugh a little.

I'll get you some of their stuff next time, I say.

Rayanne has a plate on the counter with two hot dogs. She starts piling mustard, ketchup, relish, and onions on them.

I say, Those bands you like, they're good. I downloaded some singles.

Cool, she says while putting more food on her plate.

At this point I'm pretty much out of conversation starters with a teenager. I keep focusing on her eyes.

Where's Lisa? she says.

Out there, I say.

Better rescue her.

Why?

You haven't lived here that long, Rayanne says, these people are awful. They put on faces. They always ask about school, all of them, and I'm honest and say I'm pretty crap at it, and they say that I'll do so well once I get used to it and find tons of friends, even though you can tell they're really praying their kids don't end up like me. When they're here I just go to my room and watch Hulu.

OK, I say, well why's school so crap?

I'm almost failing.

Yeah, but it seems like you really hate it.

I do.

Well why?

It's bullshit, she says.

What, class?

And the people. I don't want to make friends with the kids in my classes, and I don't care about algebra or the colonists or Huckleberry Finn.

Don't say that. I'll give you the rest, but don't talk about Huck Finn that way.

I hate that book, she says.

That book's genius, I tell her, it was huge for me in high school. And if you don't like people you should love reading Mark Twain. You'd like Kurt Vonnegut, too.

Never heard of him, she says.

I'll lend you Cat's Cradle, maybe you'll like that.

What's it about?

It's basically about how stupid people destroy the world.

Sounds like something I might like, she says.

All right, I say.

I keep feeling this need to say something important around Rayanne, to give her something she'll remember. A book, or music, or advice. Something to keep her from feeling totally mired in the nonsense of high school, to give her one thing to hang onto like I got from Dan.

It is bullshit, I say. School, it's ridiculous, you're right. I hated it, Lisa hated it. But you still have to do well if you don't want to bag up everyone's home accessories at Target for the rest of your life.

Thanks, she says.

I don't know, I say, there's a lot of crap to deal with, and you can do that or spend your whole life trying to avoid it.

OK.

Isn't there anything you want to do?

Not really, she says.

Aren't you interested in something particular?

Nope.

Lisa's chatting around the wine table with one of the women I've met once, but whose name I don't remember. The rest of the wives are in little groups, and all their husbands are scattered around the lawn, kicking the ball around with the kids.

Get lost? Lisa asks.

No, I ran into Rayanne.

Oh, the woman says, I didn't even know she was here.

I think she's holed up in her room, watching TV.

The woman says, That's like her.

Lisa and I mingle for a while longer, and leave just as some of the people start getting a little too drunk for being around their kids. A few of them start singing along with Livin' on a Prayer, which is always a good indication that it's time to go home, no matter where you are.

We say our goodbyes, agree to meet up with each couple sometime soon, and then walk back to our house.

When we walk in the cats run around our feet, clearly trying to trip us. We make it upstairs unscathed, change, and get in bed to watch some DVR'd reruns of House.

So, Lisa says, how's Rayanne?

All right, I say. She'll make some alt-boy very happy in a few years.

Why's that?

She's cool. She'll get over her angst, and she's going to be really good looking.

What does that mean?

It just means that I think she's going to be pretty when she grows up.

No, you mean hot.

Well, yeah, maybe.

She's fourteen, Nathan.

I know. I didn't tell you how smokin' she is, I said she's going to be attractive. Future tense.

Right, she says.

We did chat, you know.

Yeah, what did you two talk about?

The music I gave her.

Did she like it?

She said it was all right.

That's about as good as you're going to get, Lisa says.

And, she hates school.

Shocking. She's a teenager.

She thinks it's all bullshit, I say.

It is.

That's what I told her.

You said that?

Yeah, I told her that sometimes you just have to deal with it.

Shit, Nathan. You can't tell her things like that.

Why not?

Rayanne's not your kid.

I didn't tell her to drop out or anything. Actually, I said that she has to do better. I told her to read Huck Finn, that if she hates school she'd love Mark Twain.

Look, Lisa says, when we have a kid you can explain high school and your own Huck Finn misadventures however you want, but it's not your business to do that with someone else's daughter. I mean, does Alan seem like a guy who'd be OK with you telling Rayanne all that?

Alan doesn't seem like he's OK with anything critical.

That doesn't mean you get to mess with his parenting calls.

Right, I say.

But, she says, you can tell your dad all about this when we see him tomorrow night.

I know, he'll love it.

9
ACCIDENTAL REVOLUTION

My father and Mark Twain are somewhat responsible for my love of books. Not in the standard way, not because he read Tom Sawyer to me at night when I was a kid and made a little library for me in my room before I could even walk. He did all that, and it made me literate, but not much else.

My school district also played a role, but again, not because I had a slew of wonderful teachers who made me love great novels.

I became an avid reader because my high school did not ban The Adventures of Huckleberry Finn during my sophomore year. The superintendent of the district never used that word: banned. He explained that, although the book was taken off all curricula and removed from the school's library, no one would prevent a student from reading it on his or her own time, or even discussing it with a teacher or peer.

But, let's be honest, they banned the thing.

It happened when the mother of one of the three black students in our school—I don't know which one—complained to the teachers for the reasons you would think she'd complain. I wasn't at the PTA meeting where all this went down, but I heard from a few people that she cited Dr. King extensively. The irony that Huck is one of the first literary figures to judge someone by the content of his character rather than the color of his skin seems to have been lost on all parties.

It was lost on me, too. At that point I'd stopped reading books on adventure and exploration, and instead I was soaking in all the grunge music I could find, trying hard to ignore the rest of the world. Like all teenagers, I took myself too seriously and somehow believed I was better than everyone else with my flannel shirts, Doc Marten's, and cassettes of alt rock mixes. I couldn't have articulated why I thought I was better, I just did.

The whole banned book thing, it didn't concern me.

It concerned my father.

He's the kind of ex-hippie who went to every Grateful Dead concert in the area right up until Jerry died, but for the last ten years got luxury box seats with his friends. He will only listen to The Beatles or Janis Joplin on vinyl, the purest medium for music. He never got a tape deck component for the home stereo, and I know my mom is the only one who ever uses the CD player.

He went to law school in the seventies half to avoid the draft, and ended up founding a small firm that defends people against police misconduct, unjust discrimination, and other slightly fascist things that shouldn't happen but do all the time.

After hearing about Huck Finn, he went to the next PTA meeting and had a typical damn-the-man moment.

Again, I wasn't there, but I heard stories. In homeroom a kid tapped me on the shoulder, leaned across the aisle, and whispered that he heard my dad had flipped shit at the meeting the night before.

I told him I didn't know a thing about it.

Later that day someone else said she heard from her parents that my dad threw a fit at the meeting.

That night I asked my dad what he'd done.

I spoke my mind, he said. That's what people should do in this situation.

I told him people were saying he'd done a lot more than speak his mind.

People are blowing it way out of proportion, he said.

Here is what I pieced together from the conversations I had over the next week:

Apparently our school district had been not-banning books for years due to parental complaints, and before the PTA meeting my father got a list of the volumes teachers were prohibited from teaching and the library was forbidden from lending. How he got this I still don't know.

He purchased every book on the list and brought them to the meeting as exhibit A. He also brought the ACLU's last ten annual reports on banned books, and flyers for the ACLU of Pennsylvania's Banned Book Week festivities.

Do not fuck with a civil liberties lawyer and his son's reading list.

My father showed up at the meeting, waited patiently for the presiding officer to call on him, and then proceeded to speak for a half hour, at first with a captive audience, then over the protests of the teachers asking him to stop, then over the protests of everyone asking him to stop. He held up each of the banned books and gave a brief history of the challenges it had faced, including the Ulysses obscenity trial, the poor example for kids set by the characters in Bridge to Terabithia, and some profane and anti-patriotic passages in Slaughterhouse-Five.

When he'd finished he sat quietly back in his seat and didn't say anything else until the meeting ended and he tried handing out his flyers.

Nothing changed about the not-banned books.

You say you want a revolution, well, you know…

~

The fury after the meeting died down pretty quickly in school. Teachers must give thanks every day for the fickle nature of teenagers. I, however, was left with the complete catalogue of banned books in the Upper Derry School District, K through 12. My dad left all the books in the foyer when he came home from the PTA meeting, so I walked by them every day on my way in and out of the house.

Eventually, I got curious.

I picked up Huckleberry Finn to see what all the commotion was about and opened to the title page, which contained a notice:

PERSONS ATTEMPTING TO FIND A MOTIVE IN THIS
NARRATIVE WILL BE PROSECUTED;
PERSONS ATTEMPTING TO FIND A MORAL IN IT WILL BE BANISHED;
PERSONS ATTEMPTING TO FIND A PLOT IN IT WILL BE SHOT.

Persons attempting to find an epiphany look no further. I hadn't even read the book and the irony of the arguments at the PTA meetings became clear. Twain would have gotten a laugh out of the fights that broke out over his writing.

So I started reading the novel, and brought it to school. I was reading it at my seat before my English teacher arrived and when she did I closed the book and put it down on my desk beside my textbook. She took a long look at it.

So did a few students. Most of the kids didn't care, but a few sighed, and some shook their heads. I guess when they saw the guy who was known for being quiet and listening to his grunge tapes display the book that caused all the commotion, they viewed it more as a prank than legitimate dissent, as a way to rekindle the commotion of the debate.

No one thought that the debate had made me curious.

After class my teacher asked me to stay for a minute. She asked me what I was doing with Huck Finn.

Reading it.

She asked, Did your dad make you do that?

No.

So you just decided all by yourself to bring it in here?

Yeah.

I could tell she wanted to take it from me. I doubt she thought the book was racist, but she definitely didn't want the hassle that it brought. That's not what tenured teachers at highly rated public schools sign up for. The rules of not-banning, though, said that she couldn't do much.

She said that maybe I shouldn't leave the book out on my desk.

Maybe, I said.

She wasn't happy with that answer. The lines of her face suddenly seemed sharper, like she strained to hold something back.

I loved seeing that.

Later that day as I walked between classes, someone I didn't know yelled at me in the hallway, What the fuck is wrong with you?

A guy I knew pulled me aside before gym class and said, Do you know half the school thinks you're a racist?

What?

They all think you're in the Klan or something.

I'm Jewish, I said, I'm not in the fucking Klan. And I'm not racist either.

Well, a bunch of people think you're ready to start shit with the black kids.

That's fucked, I said.

I'm just saying, that's what they think.

For the rest of the day I got scowls in the hallways, but only from white kids.

The next day I came to my English class with the book again, and again I put it on the corner of my desk when the teacher walked in. She stared the same way, the same students glared at me. In the hallways I got some piqued looks, but no one said anything.

The following day, back in English class, I was reading the last few pages before our teacher arrived, and someone on the other side of the room said, Why are you doing that, anyway?

Reading a book?

Yes, they said, reading that book.

It's good, I said.

Which was true, I wouldn't have read the thing if it sucked. But I also got a little satisfaction in watching everyone else get upset over a book sitting on a desk, taking up very little space, and never talking out of turn.

I finished Huck Finn that evening, and the next day I came in with Slaughterhouse-Five, read it before English, placed it on my desk when class started. This time I got different looks, of annoyance and confusion rather than offense.

The racist comments stopped quickly. People just thought I was an instigator.

I liked that.

I was a teenager, I was pissed off, and when teenagers are pissed off they think everyone else should be pissed off too: How can you look at the world as it is everyday and not seethe with disgust? How can you accept the banality and mediocrity surrounding you? Well, I'll make you realize the dystopia that is suburban Philadelphia.

And I didn't want a revolution. I didn't want everyone to start agreeing with me or my dad so we could all march on the next PTA meeting. I wanted to scream my opinions in everyone's faces, have them yell back at me, and then scream again, but louder.

Thank god we all grow up.

But for a few months in high school, I loved that a Vonnegut novel on the corner of my desk angered the student body. Then Flowers for Algernon. Then Portnoy's Complaint.

The class president, a girl with a perfect GPA and an elfin body, pulled me aside one day and asked me what I was up to.

Reading, I said.

Why can't you just read those books at home? she asked.

I do read them at home. I read them here too.

Your doing that, it…it messes things up around here, Nathan.

What?

It just does, she said.

What does that even mean?

She stumbled over her words for a few seconds, and then I started again.

No one's ever been able to tell me why they hate these books so much. You don't even hate the books' content, you hate that they're near you. It's like because someone else said these books are offensive, you think you should be offended, so you act that way.

We have to respect other people's opinions, she said.

I'm not reading them out loud, I said, you tell me who I'm disrespecting.

She stood with her feet together, hands clasped in front of her. Every few seconds she rocked from her heels to her toes. I was a full head taller than her.

I have a responsibility to speak for the students, she said, and I think they don't want to be made so uncomfortable.

Then tell me who I'm making uncomfortable.

Just, maybe, think about stopping, she said, then she turned and walked away.

I don't care who's uncomfortable, I said as she went down the hallway. You don't even know why you're uncomfortable. Figure it out.

She didn't look back at me, didn't say anything else about it.

The whole thing ended when I went to see the principal. He called me in over the intercom so the entire school knew that Nathan Wavelsky should report to the Principal's Office after fourth period.

This was it, my chance to be heard, and heard through the walls by the secretaries, and maybe faintly by the kids in the classroom down the hall.

I sat across the desk from him and saw that his gray hair was tousled, his collar was undone, and his tie was loosened. His blazer was too large for him and hung off his shoulders. He leaned back in his chair before he spoke. He didn't give a crap about me.

I hear you've been reading some provocative books, he said.

I have, I said.

That has been causing some commotion.

I know, but it's not against the rules.

It is not, but that doesn't mean it's prudent.

I thought, Fuck prudence. I hope the secretaries start telling stories about the hell I'm about to raise.

The principal, who dealt with teenagers all day every day, must have known I thought something like that.

He said, I am going to ask you to stop reading those books in school. I can't make you stop, but I am going to ask, just so the focus of this high school remains on education, and not curricular decisions.

No.

Well, like I explained, I can't make you, so the decision is yours.

I'm not going to stop, I said, I think the whole thing is ridiculous.

That is your prerogative, Nathan.

Have you read those books? Can you honestly say they're too offensive to have on the curriculum?

I've read them all, he said, and there are a lot of things we leave off the curriculum for one reason or another. Then he stood up and walked around the desk, past me, and to the door. But, he said, I'm not here to discuss that with you. Then he opened the door for me.

I turned in my chair. He held out his hand, gesturing for me to leave.

That's it? I said.

What did you want? he asked.

I got up, slung my bag over my shoulder, and left. I didn't look at the principal or the secretaries on the way out.

I slipped into my chemistry class, trying not to interrupt, but of course everyone looked at me like I'd just left court.

After that no one paid much attention to my reading

habits anymore, not the teachers or the students. They all still thought I was an asshole, which I was, but they didn't mention anything to me again. Somehow, justice was done in their minds once I'd gotten a talking to.

I still wanted to have it out somehow. So I kept reading.

It took me about another two months to get through the stack of books my dad had purchased: Of Mice and Men, Howl, and finally Ulysses, which I didn't finish, but I did give it a good few weeks of effort.

And then there was nothing on the corner of my desk when English class started. All I got out of the whole thing was some ridicule and a few nice sentiments from my dad, who said he was proud of me for not being intimidated and that alone was worth everything he did.

And I got a penchant for provocative fiction: Saunders, Palahniuk, Ellis.

There was no great debate. No impassioned rhetoric. No yelling.

To this day Upper Derry High School takes books out of the curriculum and libraries, and hasn't relented on any volume, including Huck Finn.

I didn't hear about my reading habits again until graduation when, clad in cap and gown after the ceremony, someone said, Remember when you read all those banned books and pissed people off?

They weren't actually banned, I said, and raised my voice a little bit. That was the point.

Sure they were, that's why everyone was all upset.

Right, I said, whatever.

10
NO COMPLAINTS

Our parents, for all their rebellion and social upheaval in the
'60s and '70s, were still optimists. Bob Dylan warned them:
Don't follow leaders, watch the parking meters. But then The
Beatles reminded everyone that all you need is love.

Eventually, the U.S. pulled out of Vietnam.

That's not the case for us. Jeremy shot himself in front
of the class and the video ended.

And hundreds of new books get challenged every year.

So even though my wife and I like our parents, we don't
really want to hang out with them. But since we moved back
to the suburbs, a short drive from the neighborhoods where
each of us grew up, it's an obligation. Three bedrooms, quiet
neighbors, a yard, fresh air…frequent dinners with Mom and
Dad. We make that deal every time.

Tonight we're on the way to see my parents and eat
outside on the patio for the last time this year. After Alan
Gillian's birthday party yesterday, this isn't so bad—I know
how to deal with my parents. Still, Lisa tells me to be more
myself this time.

What do you mean? I ask.

You get cynical around your parents.

I tell her that I'm always cynical.

All right, she says, you get antagonistic around your

parents. Maybe just be honest with them instead of trying to outwit them.

That's not nearly so much fun, I say.

It's more fun than a pissed-off wife.

Fair enough.

The upside of seeing my mom and dad is that they drink. I wouldn't call them alcoholics, just active social drinkers, which means there's usually one moment that supplies days of conversation for Lisa and me.

Last time we ate at a French restaurant where, after two carafes, my dad flirted with the waitresses and my mom introduced herself to every other table in the place. It was embarrassing—for me at least. Lisa thought it was hilarious. So did the wait staff.

The downside is that they've never really let the dream of the '60s die. Mom, an obstetrician, has worked in a hospital from the time she graduated medical school, but when she saw the things my dad did with his firm, the people for whom he was the last line of defense, she began volunteering for Planned Parenthood. She's spent two nights a week there ever since. We used to eat at this Italian place near the clinic before her shifts so that, before she started her volunteer work, we could still have dinner together as a family.

They both led anti-Vietnam marches in college. When they show me the pictures of them in front of hundreds of protesters marching down Broad Street, I get unsettled at the mass of tie dye.

Lisa's parents are similar. Her father clerked at a grocery store to put himself through college, until he asked his boss if he could have a night off to go see The Doors. His boss said no, so he quit and went to the concert. Her mother once proudly showed me a faded picture of her holding up a flaming bra.

Now they're both accountants who spend their days figuring out ways for people to avoid giving the goddamn government any more money.

Our parents always told Lisa and me how important it is to be informed. They meant that if we're educated and up on current events, we can somehow make a difference, prevent an injustice, work for social change.

We both went to college, we read the newspapers for years, we've traveled our fair share, but in the last presidential election we voted for one of our cats, Iris, who we felt represented us more accurately than the candidates despite her lack of foreign policy experience—she's never been outside.

We show up and my dad's already into his first glass of bourbon over ice. He gives Lisa a hug and slaps me on the back, says it's good to see us. Would either of us like a drink?

Lisa asks for a gin and tonic and before I can answer my mother calls to me from the kitchen. Nathan! I need help with the wine!

She doesn't, and if she did she'd ask my dad, but I go anyway. And of course when I walk into the kitchen and give my mom a hug I see the newly opened bottle of Cabernet on the table.

She says she wants to give me something quietly, and then hands me a check for three hundred dollars. A little extra from me and dad, she says.

This happens all the time. A check, a hundred dollar bill. There's always something. And it's always supposed to be quiet, as if dad doesn't know and I'm not going to tell my wife.

Lisa's parents give us a shopping bag full of food

whenever we see them. They have our spare keys, and sometimes they leave it on our kitchen table so we get it when we come home. Often from the supermarket.

Our parents raised us to excel in school, so we could get good jobs, so we could take care of ourselves well. Now we're both thirty-two years old, we've been married four years, we make more than enough to cover our expenses—and we still get food and money from our parents. It's tough to feel grown up this way, to feel on my own, which is how I always thought they wanted me to be.

The four of us eat outside on the patio, sitting on chairs I know my father cleaned that afternoon. I flash back to when I was a kid, to when I watched him put his thumb over the hose's nozzle and spray the bird shit off the plastic outdoor furniture. They have nicer stuff now, but I'm sure he still cleans it that way before people show up.

I look out at the yard expecting to see my sheltie stalking a rabbit, but he's been dead for years. I do that every time I'm here. I loved that dog, even when he barked at the neighbors, stood in front of the TV, and somehow got fur on the clothes I hung in the closet immediately after washing them. I still expect him to come trotting over and lie under the table while we eat, hoping for a little food to fall.

Two citronella candles give the air a tangy taste, and a half dozen tea lights flicker for atmosphere.

My father starts the political discussion before anyone has passed a dish. He's on his second bourbon. He asks, Did you two hear what Senator Spencer proposed this week?

We did not.

Dad says, He wants to spend billions of dollars on

domestic surveillance programs. So, not only does he want to watch us, but who do you think will be saddled with the debt?

Who?

You two, he says, your generation.

Lisa says that sucks. Then she takes some pasta salad.

At least we might only have one year left with this guy, my dad continues. Have you thought about who you'll support in the primary?

Kilgore Trout, I say.

What?

We can't vote in the primaries, Lisa says. We're not registered with a party.

Oh, my dad says.

Once we're done eating, my mom asks us how we're doing at work.

Lisa says she's fine, that she has another month before things get crazy with early admission applications, so she wants to relax a little over the next few weeks.

Are you still taking classes? my mom asks.

I'm actually taking one right now, Lisa says, in formal epistemology.

Everyone goes quiet for a moment. Even I don't really know what that means.

It's basically the study of what knowledge is, Lisa says.

That sounds interesting, my dad says.

Mom asks, Are you close to finishing your degree?

I'm not sure about that, Lisa says, it might be something I try to do soon.

Lisa's been working in the registrar's office at St. George for long enough, and taking one philosophy class each semester she's been there, that the department has offered to award her a master's degree if she writes a thesis. She hasn't. She's told me that she doesn't even know where she'd focus in order to start writing one.

My mom continues, Don't you want to be a professor?

Maybe. I don't know, there's the whole publish or perish thing…I like taking the classes, I don't know how I'd be on the other end.

Well, Mom says, it's great that you get to do that.

I wish my parents would just out and say what they think, like most people do: what would you do with a degree in philosophy? Usually, people want to know how you'd stay solvent with that sort of degree, but my mom and dad want to know what dream it will fulfill. It's all the same to us, though, there's always got to be some other end, some great goal, which we don't have.

And now my parents ask about my job.

I tell them I had to fire someone else this week.

Oh no, my mom says, what happened?

I say, He had an error on a huge purchase order that cost the company almost a million dollars. The executives decided he had to be fired, so I fired him. That's part of my job.

Mom asks what exactly he did.

It was basically a typo, I say, one merchandise code that's only a letter different than another. And since the buyers order the other product all the time also, no one looking at the paperwork thought anything of it.

That's horrible, my mom says. Anyone could make that mistake.

Anyone could, I say. I guess the ones who don't get to keep their jobs.

I suddenly wish I'd asked for a beer instead of an iced tea. The ride home's only fifteen minutes.

My dad asks, What do you think about that?

I say, What do you mean?

You must have an opinion about the whole thing, he says.

When my boss tells me to fire a guy, I say, I try not to have an opinion.

What if all you have to say about growing up is: no complaints?

I knew someone in high school whose dad used her Bat Mitzvah to play roulette in Atlantic City. I can't say for sure, but I'll bet he hit her. She didn't have dinner at home even twice a week during school, sometimes just did her homework at a diner until it closed. She went to college in Texas and never came back.

I knew a guy in college whose parents were both law professors at Yale. One Parents Weekend his dad played pickup football with us and he could throw a perfect spiral across the quad. They took a bunch of us out to dinner and his mom told us about how President Clinton had wanted to nominate her for the Court of Appeals, but she preferred to stay at Yale and teach morning classes so she could be there when her kids got home from school.

If your mom and dad weren't any of that, then you get to this point: where dinner with them is stunted conversation, where the people who raised you for all those years don't understand you anymore.

And that's OK. It has to be.

Graham Nash told them to feed us on their dreams.

The Cranberries told us that your dream's never quite as it seems.

~

Lisa and I stay for dessert and coffee, then say that we have to leave.

Well, we all have to work tomorrow, my mom says.

The four of us get up and walk from the patio around the house to our car in the driveway. My dad walks slowly and motions that I should as well. He puts his arm around my shoulder and squeezes a little more tightly than I'd like. He had a generous glass of port after dinner.

He says, Are you happy, Nathan?

His tone reminds me of the Are You Ready? talk we had before I left for Montcrief, and the Are You Nervous talk we had before my wedding.

Sure, I say.

I mean, is this where you wanted to be?

So I think about that for a second. My teachers always said I could do whatever I wanted, shuffled me and my classmates into assemblies where we listened to Upper Derry alumni talk about becoming bankers, lawyers, pilots, economists... My parents bought me career guides before and after college, told me there wasn't a single option in those books I couldn't excel in, all I had to do was find what inspired me.

I say, I never really wanted to be anywhere in particular.

You're smart, he says, I want to make sure that if there's something you want for yourself, you get it.

It's OK to not care about politics, I think. It's fine if you don't want to help people or change the world.

My dad tells me he still gets a lot of gratification knowing he was part of a movement that, at least a little bit, changed society. That those ideas stick with him today.

I remind myself that it's not a crime to be asocial. That you don't have to fix anything about anyone else.

Dad says that maybe I should think a little about my passion, that if I want it's not too late to change course a little and shoot for something else. He says he knows how hard it can be, but he and Mom would support me.

I think about how maybe a job doesn't have to involve fighting for something or solving society's ills. Maybe there's nothing greater than my shelf of books, my old scratched CDs, my yard, my cats, and my wife.

I tell my dad that I think I'm OK, but thanks for being there.

I put the car in gear and back out of the driveway. While my parents are still waving to us I say, That wasn't so bad.

Did you tell your dad about Rayanne and Huck Finn?

No, I say.

Why not?

It means something different to him than it does to me. He thinks of it as fighting the system. I mean, you heard what he said today about senators and primaries and how we're going to have all the debt. I don't want to get in more conversations like that than I have to.

You don't think he'd want to know that you remember it all, that you're passing the book on to someone else now?

He wouldn't see it as something so simple as recommending a cool book, he'd make it into some socio-political thing.

OK, Nathan. But shouldn't you at least tell them about watching Rayanne that night?

Why?

We did something neighborly, she says, took someone into our home we didn't really know.

For a night.

Still, your parents would want to know we did that.

I don't think it's really newsworthy.

Yes it is, she says.

We drive for a few more minutes and then Lisa says, Kilgore Trout? Really?

What? I say.

They don't get it, she says, they don't get you—I understand that. But if you don't want to talk to your dad about politics and the system, why don't you just tell him instead of being a smart ass?

I tell her that her parents don't get her either.

They don't, she says. But I don't fight it. You shouldn't either.

I know. By the way, my mom gave me a check for three hundred dollars.

Really?

Yeah, I say. She told me it's something extra.

What do they think we are?

Same thing they always have, I say, their kids.

11
CAT'S CRADLE

I open the door and see Alan Gillian on my doorstep.

Hey Alan, I say.

Hello Nathan.

He's angry. He's contorted his face and narrowed his eyes in that way a guy does when you've joked about something he'll never find funny, like his job, his grandmother, his clothes— every guy has something, but you don't know what it is until you step on it.

He is holding the copy of Cat's Cradle I gave to Rayanne.

You gave this to my daughter, he says as he holds up the paperback.

Shit, he's adopting that angry principal tone.

Yeah, I say, I thought she'd like it.

She did, he says.

Oh, well, what's up then?

I don't.

You don't...like the book?

No.

Oh, I say. Well, I'm sorry about that. It's pretty good, though, you might want to give Vonnegut another chance.

We're a Christian family, Nathan.

I think, Crap.

When he first knocked I was on my couch watching

The Big Lebowski on cable. I have the DVD, but there are some movies you'll always watch when you find them on TV. Even if you own them. Even if they're on a station where all the profanity's edited out. The Godfather, The Great Escape, Reality Bites. The Dude was bowling when Alan knocked, and I almost paused the live TV, but I didn't. Now I'm thinking that this conversation will last well past my favorite scene, in Maude Lebowski's art studio.

Alan says, I don't want this sort of book in my house, I don't want this sort of influence for my daughter.

OK, I say, I understand your feelings, but let's not blow this out of proportion.

With my family and my home, he says, I cannot take this too seriously.

I begin to realize just how awful I am at recognizing an important event as it's happening.

While Alan's talking and the winter air begins drifting into my house, I piece together the moments that led to this. I think it begins with the library.

It makes sense to finish the bedroom, the living room, or even the kitchen when you first move into a new home. Lisa and I did the library. Before we bought a dining room table or a new TV we spent a weekend picking out bookshelves, pictures, chairs, and a desk, all of which we used to turn one of the three bedrooms into our oasis of literature. Most people who see it would call it a home office, but we don't do much more than pay bills at the desk—the stacks of books by each chair, and empty mugs stained with coffee and tea tell you more about what we use the room for.

When it comes to home libraries, I have a leather

couch Victorian study aesthetic. Lisa likes the ultra-modern minimalist approach. We ended up with black bookshelves along the whole of the two long walls in the rectangular room, a small chestnut desk under the window on the back wall, and two plush chairs in the center. We put an iHome on top of one of the shelves, but we never use it. The window opens up on to the front yard and our street, which isn't busy, and keeping it cracked provides plenty of white noise for us.

Organizing the books was a fun afternoon. We decided to put the thick hardback books, mostly intro. to philosophy textbooks and Norton literature anthologies, on the top shelves where they looked good but stayed out of reach since there's no reason for opening them ever again. Then we went by genre: mysteries, cozies, modernists, mountains, sci-fi, beloved childhood volumes, books we bought abroad, books required in school we couldn't sell back, books bought for us we'll read soon, books bought for us we have no intention of reading, books we want to read but which are too long for a commitment with our current schedules... We're not really done with this organization, and I doubt we ever will be, but that's one great part about it.

We sit in there on Saturday and Sunday mornings, during days off, and whenever we otherwise get a chance. It's funny, but I rarely find myself in there without Lisa. It's our room, and neither of us like being in it by ourselves, but together there's almost nowhere else in Pennsylvania we'd want to be.

Just after my indignant neighbor's birthday party and about a month before he appears at my front door—where he's still talking at me—Rayanne showed up in my back yard. By all that's normal, on that day my books should have still been in boxes on the floor of the future Wavelsky library and my kitchen should have had fresh paint or new wallpaper. Had that been the case, none of this would have happened.

However...

I was drinking green tea on my patio after work and I heard what I thought was a Harley pull up outside our house, which is pretty unusual in this neighborhood. I got up and walked around to the front yard where I saw a green Chevy Impala from the late '80s parked outside the Gillians' house, one that had no muffler to speak of. I watched it for a moment and then saw Rayanne crawl out the passenger side. It roared off once she got to the sidewalk.

I turned to go back to the patio, but she said, Hi. I waved to her, and then she started walking across her lawn toward my house. She had an army surplus jacket on, and a faded Bad Religion t-shirt underneath. Her jeans were split open at the knees.

My English teacher mentioned that guy you like, she said. The V guy.

Vonnegut? I said.

Yeah, him.

Did your teacher assign any of his books?

She just mentioned him for some reason, Rayanne said, but I recognized the name.

I said, What reason?

She said she wasn't paying much attention in class, that the name just caught her ear.

I wanted to start a lecture on Vonnegut's writing, but then remembered that I was talking to a fourteen-year-old. So I just said, That's cool.

Yeah, she said.

And then I offered to lend Rayanne one of his books.

As soon as she mentioned Vonnegut I envisioned the cracked blue spine with the red block letters on the second shelf from the bottom, towards the left, in the satire section, subcategory: biting.

It seemed only natural to let her borrow it, not like an event.

I invited her in, offered her a soda, which she declined, then walked her upstairs to the library where I pulled out my old paperback copy of Cat's Cradle with the stained pages and curled up corners and said, Here, this is a good one to start with.

She took it, said thanks, put it in her bag, and then I walked her to the door. She wasn't in the house for five minutes.

Actually, I don't want to say that I was so cavalier about giving her the book, I felt good about it. A little like a teacher, or a mentor. Helping a kid, one who's kind of like Lisa and I used to be, to get through those disgruntled years.

That's not how her father sees it.

So it goes.

I wasn't listening to Alan while I traced the origin of this lecture, so I pick it up at him asking, Do you go to church?

I'm Jewish, I say.

He asks if I go to synagogue.

No, I say.

I want to tell him that my Judaism more or less rests on the fact that I have an inexplicable love for matzah, but now's probably not the right time.

Well, he says, we go to church. Not as much as I'd like, but that's my fault. We do go, Nathan, and I think it's important for my daughter to have positive influences like our congregation, our pastor, and our God.

I think about how seven or eight years ago this would have been a seriously enjoyable fight for me, attacking all his ideas of faith, trying to score a victory for atheism. I still have an inclination to jump into it, to ask him just how Christian it is to go to a dinner event on a weeknight instead of spending time with his family, to have him tell me whether or not Jesus would have downed a six pack with the apostles on his birthday, but I resist it. Arguing about religion is pretty sad. Aside from the fact that it's impossible to win when having it out with a true believer, all I have to offer someone in exchange for a god who loves them is a cold, random, uncaring universe. I don't even want to change their minds, really.

OK, I tell Alan, I'm sorry about all this.

I don't want you to give anything else to Rayanne, he says, she has enough problems.

Come on, Alan, I don't think a fourteen-year-old reading a novel is really a problem.

He snaps. He says, Stay away from my daughter.

I feel myself taking a small step back into my house, purely by instinct.

All right, I say.

He holds out the book to me and I take it. Slowly.

Oh, he says, I also have this for you.

He pulls out the USB stick I gave to Rayanne, the one with all the music on it.

I think this is yours, he says.

He tosses it at me, and I try to catch it with one hand but I can't. It drops between my feet.

He's a little older than me, but I'll bet Alan was one of those fuckers who listened to Jars of Clay.

I reach down and pick up the thumb drive, and when I

stand up Alan's saying, Goodbye, Nathan. Then he turns and walks away, taking the little paved path across my front lawn to the sidewalk and back to his house.

I go back to the couch, toss the stick onto my coffee table, and resume my movie watching—Walter and the Dude are in a coffee shop arguing about toe-nail polish—but I find myself glancing back at that stupid thumb drive sitting by my glass of water. It wasn't like the backpacks full of CDs I borrowed from Dan, Jon, and Adelle's rooms, or the stacks of tapes I used to copy them. Rayanne never asked for the music, I'm not even sure she liked it. But that's what I thought of when I gave her the songs and the book.

Clearly, things have changed.

12
NESTING

I come home from work and find a new, sleek, glass-top end
table from Crate & Barrel next to my couch. I know the store
because Lisa left the empty box in the corner of the room, next
to the brown boxes full of board games and old cat toys which
had, for the few months since we moved and until today, been
serving as our end table, and serving well I thought.

All our unwashed glasses and bowls from this morning
have been cleared off the coffee table, as have the stack of
magazines and the thumb drive I left there a few days ago.

Also, the house smells awful.

The hell? Not that we can't afford the table, or that I
mind getting out of a trip to a housewares store and coming
home to a clean living room, but we usually do this sort of
shopping together.

I can't watch a movie without my neighbor telling me I've
corrupted his daughter, and now I clearly can't have my tea on
the patio. Strange few days.

Lisa, I call. Hun, are you home?

She answers that she's upstairs in the guest bedroom.

I walk up and see some plastic Home Depot bags scattered
in the upstairs hallway. Then I recognize the smell: paint.

Lisa's in an old pair of jeans and a white tank top with a
roller in hand and cans of dark yellow paint on the floor, one

of which is open. She's draped sheets over the bed, but not over the carpet. I don't see a paint tray.

Um, I say, what's up?

The house needs to be finished, she says.

Right. But, today?

I have to go back to this morning for a minute. I was on the couch, dressed for work, eating a bowl of cereal with one hand while holding The Joke by Milan Kundera with the other, and wondering how The Unbearable Lightness of Being is more famous.

Then Lisa came downstairs and I heard, I hate that empty bedroom.

Shut the door, I said, then you won't have to look at it.

When I see the closed door, I'll just remember why we keep it closed. We need to paint it and get some furniture.

OK.

Seriously, Nathan, I want to do this.

Right, I said. We'll go to the store this weekend and check out paints and things.

Why can't we buy paint? she said.

We can, I said, but you'll want the paint to go with the furniture we buy. So we'll have to go to Ikea or wherever and figure that out too, right? Then we can buy it all. Might take a few days.

Yeah, she said, but we need to actually do it.

We will. This weekend, or next. Soon, hun.

OK, she said. Then she sat down next to me.

What's your day like today? she asked.

Nothing spectacular, I said. Conference call at 10:00, lunch meeting with the marketing people—I don't know why they send me to those things, I have no idea about that stuff—and some evaluations of the new staff in the afternoon.

Do you have to put on a tie for any of that?

No, I said. I could even get away with jeans and a decent shirt, I think, but khakis are safer. They make me look like I'm trying.

Are you?

If you consider relying on common sense trying. What about your day?

The office is pretty dead right now, she said. We've got all the mid-year transfers done, so right now it's all getting ready for the flood of applications for next year. A lot of the staff is on vacation, so I think it'll be slow until after New Year's.

Bring a book to work, I told her.

I always do, and anyway I have to study for my epistemology final next week.

Then I finished my cereal, which got a little soggy while Lisa and I talked, kissed her goodbye and went to work.

Once I got in the car and plugged in my iPod I forgot about that conversation. The ones with implications are never the ones that linger in my mind.

There have been mornings when Lisa and I yell at each other and leave without resolving anything. I'll think about that all day, expecting it to continue once we get home, but then we'll walk in the door, have a hug, and laugh as we try to figure out why we were so mad about forgetting to buy something at the market or not doing the laundry the night before.

Painting the guest bedroom…that didn't register at all on the Potential To Irrevocably Change My Marriage scale, which apparently needs to be recalibrated.

~

Now, though, I'm watching my wife try to paint. I'm watching her fuck it up pretty badly, too. She hasn't gotten any on the walls yet, but half a roller's soaked in paint—she dipped it straight in the can. It's lying on a plastic bag on top of the carpet. A little pool is forming which, if there's a rip in that bag, will make this job much bigger.

This needs to be done, she says.

Why now?

Because we keep putting it off.

How did you get all this stuff today?

I took the day off work, she says. I didn't have to be there, and classes are over, so I thought it'd be a better use of my time to finish our home.

Did you ask for help?

Well, you had those meetings—

No, I say, did you ask for help when you bought the paint?

I googled it, she says.

OK, well, you're going to kill the cats. Or at least get them high.

I walk to the window and open it, letting in the cold gusts which have been whistling through the shut windows since this morning. Then I go to the paint cans and put the top back on the open one.

Did you buy a paint tray? I ask.

No, Lisa says.

Well, I say, you have rollers but no tray, which will make things a little difficult. And then you got two wall brushes but no trim brushes. I don't even know if this room needs to be scraped or primed before we paint it, and if it does I don't know how to do that. So, hun, maybe we should wait until this weekend.

She's frustrated. She's been manic since I got here, so I guess telling her to stop isn't going to go over well.

How do you know all this? she asks.

You grow up with my father, I say, you pick things up. How to hang a picture, how to chop wood, how to paint a wall.

She strides out of the room, taking an exaggerated step over the half-wet roller. I walk over to the cans and pick one up to read the label: Mustard Yellow latex house paint, water based. Then I pick up the roller and see that the half without paint is wet with water, as it should be when you're going to use it with latex paint.

I put the top back on the can of paint, then go into our bedroom and hear Lisa washing up in the bathroom. The door's locked.

When she comes out I see that a few locks of her hair have fallen over her face, the ends almost tickling her jawline. She's wearing sneakers I thought she'd thrown out. Her jeans are ripped at the upper thigh. First I think that's sexy, teasing me with a smooth little patch of skin I'd love to run my fingertips along, then I think about how cute it'll be when we actually do paint and she ends up with a little birthmark of yellow on the top of her leg. I sit down on the bed, hoping she's going to come over and kiss me, which will lead to a little mid-week sex. Instead, she goes to the dresser to change into her old college sweat pants and puts on one of my hoodies.

So, I ask, what inspired the shopping day?

I can't fucking stand what we've done with this house, she says.

Why? We picked everything out together.

We haven't done shit. We've been here for five months, Nathan, and until today we had a hobo's table next to our couch, a bedroom that makes a summer camp cabin look ritzy, and no plan for any of it. We've got a stove, a dishwasher, and a washer/dryer that came with the place because the last owners didn't want them anymore.

Yeah, I say, but those things still work fine.

Who gives a shit if they work, she says, they're not fucking ours.

It is, at this moment, that I realize the full gravity of the situation. I'm still on the edge of the bed, Lisa's standing in front of me in sweats, arms akimbo, looking determined enough to successfully invade a small European principality.

Lisa, I say, sweetheart, it takes time to redo all this stuff.

I know it takes time, but we haven't even talked about it. You put your mug on those boxes every goddamn day and never even think about a table being better. You boil water on that shit stove and never consider that a new one—one that we like—would make a difference.

You did?

Of course I did.

Why didn't you say anything?

Do I have to tell you that we should have a table instead of a stack of boxes? Do I have to tell you our spare room where my sister will sleep, if I ever have a house I want to invite her to, shouldn't be a spartan cell? Do I have to tell you that we're in our thirties and we should have a home instead of an enclosed space with a roof?

We do have a home, I say, our kind of home.

This isn't my kind of home, she says.

OK, well, I'm fine with making the place nicer. You know that. But it's a little hard for me to get going with it when you spend the day buying stuff and don't talk to me about what you want.

I just don't see how the house hasn't made you crazy up till now, she says.

It didn't seem to make you crazy before today.

Well, it did.

Right, I say. Maybe next time, though, just tell me how you feel.

She lets her arms fall and sits next to me on the bed. I put my arm around her shoulders and gently pull her back so we're both lying flat with our legs dangling over the edge. Lisa's tearing, but not crying, and I try running my fingers through her hair to calm her down a little.

She says, Do you know that I cried the other day when I saw two mothers with their strollers? It wasn't conscious, like: Wow, I wish I had a baby, then a pain in my uterus, then bawling. I was at a red light, saw the women, waited for the signal to turn green, accelerated, got almost a full mile down the road, then all out crying. I couldn't figure it out for a few minutes, but then I remembered the babies—which only made it worse. I pulled over a few blocks from the house so I could compose myself before I came in.

I feel all my digestive organs clench in unison.

Wow, I say.

I feel like a crazy person, she says.

Yeah, well, that's pretty intense.

What do you think about all this?

About you being a crazy person?

No, she says, about a home and a family.

I definitely want to work on the house, I say. Maybe plan things out a little better, but we'll get it done. And, I know you've been thinking about kids, but what about school and finishing your thesis?

I haven't even started a thesis.

But you will. I mean, can you do that with kids?

Forget about my academics for a minute. Forget everything and do a thought experiment: what do you think about starting a family?

I don't know. I have a lousy history with babies.

You have no history with babies, she says.

I do. Remember when we were dating and we went to my cousin Reuben's kid's bris? We were on the couch with my mom before it all started, and Reuben came over and handed the baby to me, except I don't know how to hold one. The thing's legs were dangling and it started crying until my mom took it and calmed it down.

OK, Lisa says, that must have been a traumatic thirty seconds for you, but it doesn't mean you're bad with children. That was almost seven years ago, anyway, how do you even remember it?

I just do.

Well, you'll learn.

I'll what?

You'll learn, she says.

Then she gets up and puts her arms in the air to stretch so her shirt lifts up and I can see her midriff for a second. I think about sex again, it only takes a little exposed patch to make me think about how delicious the rest is.

Let's go downstairs, she says. What do you want for dinner?

Whatever, I say, I'm still a little stuck on the whole you'll learn thing.

Look, Nathan, you're just the kind of guy who has kids. You're smart, nice, stable...prime father material. Look at how you are with Rayanne.

Good enough that her father wants me to stay away from her.

Alan's crazy, she says, anyone else would love a neighbor who encourages their teenage kid to read classic novels.

Maybe, I say.

I mean, I never thought about you as a father when we decided to get married, but the idea must have been in me somewhere. I think it's one of the reasons I like you so much. Subconsciously, I mean.

Until now, I say. Now it's all right out there.

Yeah, until now.

13
MISUNDERSTANDING

What the fuck did you do?

Lisa slams the front door behind her, and her heels click on the hardwood floor.

Nathan!

I've just washed my mug after drinking tea on the patio—at least this time I got to finish what I was doing. My cheeks and nose are a little raw from the cold.

I'm in the kitchen, I say.

This is going to be bad, way worse than the end table and painting thing last week. She's come into the house angry before, but never yelling from two rooms away, never on a trajectory for me before even taking off her shoes.

She walks in, tosses her purse on one of the chairs, and throws her coat on the table, knocking off some of the mail that's piled up there. Her shoes are still on and I'm worried the heels might break through the floor the way she's coming toward me.

She says, What did you do with Rayanne?

What do you mean?

I mean you did something to weird out our neighbors.

Oh yeah, I say, I told you about Alan Gillian coming by.

You told me he was pissed about you loaning Rayanne a book and giving her some music.

He was.

Well, she says, that's not why Kristy Harrison ignored me in the supermarket a half hour ago.

I think, Since when is Kristy Harrison ignoring you a bad thing?

I say, I don't know why Kristy Harrison ignored you.

Lisa tells me she saw her in the produce section, and when she said hello Kristy looked away, towards the cantaloupes. Lisa stepped over to her and said hello again, Kristy forced a smile, quietly said hi, and then moved her cart towards the next aisle. Lisa caught up with her and asked what the problem was. Kristy said, Nothing. Lisa pressed her. Kristy said, It's just… We saw Rayanne go in your house one afternoon, then Alan told Tom and me about your husband and her, and, well, it disturbs us. Lisa asked what disturbed her, and all Kristy said was, That kind of relationship. Then she pushed her cart away and Lisa didn't follow.

What the fuck is she talking about? Lisa asks.

I don't know.

What kind of relationship do you have with Rayanne?

The kind where I lend her books and music.

And where you think about how hot she's going to be.

Oh come on—

Is it also the kind where you invite her into our house when I'm not home?

Yeah, I say, to give her a book.

You didn't tell me that part of the story, she says, you didn't tell me she came in here with you. How do you think that looks?

I don't know, I say, polite?

It looks like you're a fucking creep, Nathan, like you ought to be registering on some database and knocking on everyone's door when you move to notify them you're in the neighborhood.

You can't be serious, I say.

I am. Don't you read the news at all?

You know I don't.

Honestly, she says, you walk the Earth every day, you have to know that everyone's hyper worried about their kids getting abused or molested.

OK, yeah.

So how could you take her in the house when you were home alone?

I didn't know I was being watched, I say.

Really? As many people live in our neighborhood now as lived in our building in the city. Everybody knows what everyone else does. And besides, it's just creepy.

No it's not, I say. OK, assuming I was being watched by the whole street, it would be creepy if she were nine years old, but Rayanne's in high school, and she was only in the house for a few minutes. And she left with a book. What exactly would someone think I did in that situation, have my way with her for ninety seconds, catch my breath, then give her some Vonnegut as a parting gift?

You know, she says, none of that matters now that people have the idea in their heads.

It fucking should, I say.

It doesn't, she says.

Then Lisa walks upstairs and closes the door as she changes out of her work clothes. She makes dinner, and we eat it on the couch in front of Jeopardy, but neither of us offer too many answers. Even the cats are on the couch next to her instead of me.

~

The next day I pull my car into the driveway after work, get out, and jog down towards my mailbox. It's cold, but I don't bother putting on my coat to walk thirty yards and back. I see the Beales, an older couple from the other end of the block, walking their dog on the sidewalk and I wave. They make eye contact with me, but don't gesture, and pick up their pace as they pass my property. For a minute as I stand with my mail in my hand, which gets numb with cold, all I hear is the jingling of the dog's tags as they go by.

I let Lisa start the conversation at dinner, and she says a few things about looking over the first batch of applicants for the university, then mentions that we need to go to The Container Store and get some storage baskets for under our bed. She's curt, and doesn't laugh at my jokes, or the ones on TV.

A day later it's 7:30 am and I stop at a Starbucks on my way to work. I have a conference call with the Sirs at 8:00, and I need a triple grande latte with a few shots of something sugary before I'll have the cognitive capacity to deal with that. After I order I walk to the end of the bar and wait for the barista to put my drink up and yell my name in my ear. She's just started steaming my milk when the cashier calls out the next customer's drink, and Tom Harrison walks over to wait for his nonfat sugar-free caramel macchiato.

I nod to him, and get ready to put out my hand, but he goes and leans against the window. He definitely sees me.

So I take a few steps over to him.

Tom, I say, what's up?

He picks his eyes up to me and again, for one of the few times in my life, I feel tall. He says, I've never seen you here, Nathan.

Yeah, I say, early meeting, I need a little caffeine.

He says, Oh.

You all right? I ask.

I'm fine, he says. Then he lowers his eyes again.

Hey, what's wrong?

Do you really want to talk about it here?

Talk about what?

Don't be like that, he says, you know what.

You mean the thing Kristy mentioned to Lisa?

Yes.

You have it all wrong, I just loaned Rayanne a book. That's all.

But what kind of book? Tom says.

A good one.

It's nothing a teenager should be reading, he says.

That confuses me for a moment.

No, I say, it's exactly what a teenager should be reading.

Alan told us it's a lewd novel, and I'm pretty sure he should make the decisions about what his daughter reads.

I think, Not if he's a cretin.

Well, I say, the book's got a cynical edge to it, sure, but... wait, Alan told you? Have you read Cat's Cradle?

I'm afraid I've never looked at it.

The barista screams my name and I flinch a bit. I take two steps to the counter and grab my cup, which is hot even through the post-consumer recycled sleeve. Then I turn back to Tom but he's already on his Blackberry, scrolling through emails. He's sliding his finger across the screen so fast there's no way he's actually reading anything.

Tom, I say, there's been a misunderstanding here.

He says, I don't want to get into it. Alan's my friend, and I'm just trying to support him.

Come on, I say, you can't know what you're supporting unless you listen to me, or at least read the book.

The barista calls Tom's drink.

I'm finished talking about this, he says as he grabs his cup.

All right, I say.

I let him walk out first, far enough ahead of me that he doesn't have to hold the door. As I get into my car I think, Sheep, but then reprimand myself.

The call with the Sirs, about storage and shipping logistics, is like having a corkscrew turned into my temple—it is painful and something essential drains out of me.

When I get home after work I take my tea to the patio and look at the spruces lining my yard, at the bare branches of the maple towering over the house behind mine, at the Harrisons' pin oak which looks like it has a coating of frost instead of leaves. I didn't bring gloves out so I use my mug to keep my hands warm. When the tea's done I shove my hands in the pockets of my pea coat and lean forward in my chair.

Except for the few passing cars, I only hear the evergreen needles brushing against each other in the light breezes. I don't get up until Lisa pulls her car into the driveway. Then I go inside to meet her, and when she sees me she asks why my face is so red.

I tell her that I was having my tea on the patio. She says that I should spend a little less time out there in the winter.

Probably, I say, but I like the cold.

The cold makes your skin angry, she says.

I think that I'm married and I don't care too much anymore.

We both go upstairs and change into hoodies and sweatpants, then I follow Lisa to the kitchen where she starts chopping vegetables for a stir-fry dinner.

I lean against the table and tell her that I saw Tom Harrison at Starbucks that morning.

Oh, she says, and is he still your buddy?

No, I say, he thinks I'm a creep trying to corrupt Rayanne.

She stops moving the knife and looks at me like she's expecting me to finish.

I tried to talk about it with him, I say, but he just said he supports his friend who thinks Cat's Cradle is a lewd book, which it isn't. Critical, yes, but lewd, not really.

She says, Do you really think this is about literary criticism?

No, I say.

I shift my weight a little but there's no way for me to get comfortable.

I say, the Beales ignored me yesterday while they walked their dog past the house.

Really? she says as she resumes chopping.

Yeah, the sweet old Beales.

How about that, she says, then moves the vegetables to the side before taking out the chicken to cut that up.

I'm sorry, I say, I shouldn't have given her that book.

OK, she says.

She turns on the burner and gets out three bottles of sauce for the food. I see that this isn't quite resolved. All husbands know that it's not enough to apologize, you have to correctly articulate what you're apologizing for.

There's nothing illicit about the whole thing, I say. I'm just thinking about Dan and Jon, my high school friends, how they showed me all the stuff I ended up loving.

Were your high school friends in their thirties? she asks.

No.

Then it's not really the same, she says, is it?

She takes the cutting board and spills everything into the wok. The kitchen fills with hissing and popping.

We wanted to make a life here, she says over all the noise. We wanted to come here and have our home for years and years. I'm trying to build that for us, and just when I think we have the same ideas about everything, about how to build a home, I find out that you did your thing and fucked it all up. In six months, Nathan.

I'm sorry, I say.

You need to think about where we are, she says.

I know, I say. And I did think about it. It was gratifying, giving her the music, the book. Maybe she didn't actually read it, or listen to those songs, but I like that she might have, that maybe I did something cool for her.

Lisa mixes the stir-fry. It's a little quieter now.

She says, That's nice, hun. Which doesn't mean it's OK.

Yeah, I say, no kidding.

You know when you can do all that?

When common sense returns to suburbia?

No, she says. Are you listening to what you're saying? About giving someone else the things you love?

Sure, I say.

I don't think you are, I don't think you see just how

you've been acting towards her. Doesn't it make you look a little bit more toward our future?

How?

She comes over and gives me a kiss. A long kiss, but more like how Michael kissed Fredo after he betrayed the family than a wife who's forgiven me.

She says, Everything we've been talking about, does it look a little different at all now?

That's a lot to take in, I tell her.

Well you've had your time, she says as she turns back to the wok, you should start wrapping your head around it about now. And bring some silverware and glasses of water downstairs, dinner will be ready soon.

14
LA LA LOVE YOU

Lisa and I fell in love during our junior year at Montcrief, in a course on dystopian novels.

I was a communications major, because I liked to read but I wanted a chance at a job after graduation. Lisa was a philosophy major because she liked to read and figured college was the last time she'd have a chance to do that all she wanted and get something out of it, even if it was just a diploma. We both took the class as an elective.

The professor was pretty demanding, asking for a three page essay every Friday and assigning us a novel to read each week, so a few students got a study group together for the mid-term which we all knew would be a bitch. After class ended one day they asked both of us to join.

Lisa said, No thanks, then she continued packing up her things.

I asked when it was.

Thursday night, they said. And then maybe again over the weekend

Um, I said.

Some of these people were in two other classes with me, and probably would be for the next few years. I told them to send me an email, I'd probably go.

Lisa and I got on the elevator together a few minutes later.

You don't want to go to that study group, do you? she asked.

What? No, I mean, it'll be helpful.

Maybe, but do you want to spend a night talking about The Handmaid's Tale with them?

Not really, I said, but they're in my other classes and this test is going to be awful, so maybe it's a good idea.

They're not your cousins, she said, don't worry about offending them. Unless you want to spend more time listening to Lacanian, Foucauldian, postmodern...whatever.

That Thursday night we went on our first date at a bar that only served beer microbrewed on the premises and had hundreds of bobble head dolls as decoration, which we thought were creepy and endearing at the same time. Lisa and I have gone back to this bar every year on our dateaversary.

I remember the host showing us to our table, letting Lisa walk in front of me, and thinking about the skirt and boots she had on, how for some reason I found women in that kind of outfit so sexy and had not until that night been on a date with one who wore it.

We tried a pint of each type of beer until we got a little too drunk for a first date. She reached across the table and ran her hand through my hair, which was much longer then. She said that she loved my curls, and I finally had a reason to be thankful for the frizzy mass on my head. I told her that I didn't mind a pretty girl touching it. She got up and moved her chair around the table and we sat right beside each other for the rest of the night.

And we kept drinking until we started mentioning the things that you usually keep hidden until someone likes you enough to accept them.

Lisa told me she had her VCR set to record Daria every week, and kept the tapes hidden from her roommate just in case.

I told her that the new advertising campaign for some brand of soda which said it was the coldest tasting drink in the world drove me nuts. How can you taste temperature?

She said that when the Alanis Morissette single Ironic came out she made a Book of Actual Irony for her friends who got confused by the song.

I admitted that I owned, and on occasion wore, a t-shirt that said: Welcome To Philadelphia, Now Go Home.

These little peccadilloes can end a first date—or make it into the best first date you've ever had.

The next week we both passed the mid-term.

Lisa and I stayed together through the rest of college. I gave her a copy of Breakfast of Champions, she introduced me to Under the Net.

We discovered that our favorite times in Philadelphia were Memorial Day and Labor Day weekends because almost everyone goes down the shore, so we could eat at any restaurant in peace and quiet.

We shared a mutual disgust for people who use gauge earrings to stretch their lobes down to their shoulders.

We went to one poetry reading. The author walked onto the small stage, adjusted the mic, and announced that she would be reading from her new collection called Rape Garden. We downed our drinks, walked out, and never went to another one again.

We stayed in Philadelphia after graduation, in a one bedroom apartment in the Bella Vista section, and in a lot of ways our lifestyles didn't change. Neither of us were National Merit

Scholars or Phi Beta Kappa members—we always studied, but refused to end up in the college's counseling office because we had anxiety attacks over a B.

This is also the way we treated our jobs. We worked hard in the office, but tried not to think about it when we got home.

It wasn't that we didn't aspire to a promotion, it's that we didn't aspire to anything. We were the kids who heard their public school teachers tell them that they could be anything, even President of the United States; whose parents insisted that we would be the generation to change the world; who grew up in the age where everyone's special.

Then we looked at the politicians, our teachers, our peers.

And we said, Horseshit.

And we were happy.

We got our news from the Daily Show and The Onion. We liked the idea of recycling and hybrid cars not because we were terribly worried about the ozone layer, but because pollution smells bad. In 2004 we concerned ourselves less with the race between John Kerry and George Bush than we did with getting tickets for the Pixies reunion tour.

This all comes with awkward moments, like when you're waiting for your boss to show up to a managers' meeting and someone asks you what you think about the governor of New Jersey coming out of the closet, and you reply with a genuine, Huh?

The thing that's been consistent for Lisa and me is travel. From our first paychecks after graduation, we've budgeted for a trip each year the way most people budget for their retirement funds. Camping and hiking with Mark became foreign adventures with my wife, and those experiences have confirmed our relationship annually.

We went to Italy where we trained between Rome, Florence, and the Amalfi Coast. Both of us tried copious amounts of wine of all different varieties, and while Lisa came out of that with a refined palate, I came out with a headache, knowing only the difference between red and white. We saw several Madonna and Child paintings by Raphael at the Borghese Gallery, and left wondering why he painted his lord and savior to look like a baby who had just downed a fifth of vodka and groped at his mother's chest. We watched a football match in an Amalfi bar over Limoncello and Birra Moretti, and when the local team won in extra time hundreds of people ran through the main square and threw themselves into the ocean to celebrate. Lisa and I then found ourselves in a deserted bar. Even the bartender and waitress were splashing around in the surf.

A year later we went to Scotland and visited scotch whiskey distilleries—that time I came out with the developed taste while Lisa had the headache. We went to a folk music pub in Edinburgh where we listened to fiddlers and guitarists improvise for hours, and had a very drunk Scotsman insist that we Americans had defaced the game. We asked which game he meant, and he said, Rugby. Then to show there were no hard feelings he bought Lisa and me a round, but when he took a sip of his own pint he turned green and bolted out of the pub. He never came back.

We love those moments, you couldn't make them up.

Five years after graduation we got married and honeymooned in Japan. I'd noticed that Lisa was talking at length about her newly engaged office secretary, and I saw her taking some longer-than-usual looks when we passed the

Tiffany's on Walnut Street. I bought her a ring—Tiffany's style—and proposed. The night before our wedding she gave me a watch, an Omega Speedmaster, the kind astronauts wore on the moon. She said that if it worked on the moon, it ought to work anywhere we go.

Japan is the most foreign place we'd ever been, and I think brought us closer together than standing under a fancy tent, trading rings, and smashing a glass.

Nice Japanese restaurants often have set menus, and almost always have traditional settings, which include sitting on tatami mats and removing your footwear at the door. By the end of our trip this is how we summed up eating in Japan: You will not be able to wear your shoes, you will not be given a chair, and you will eat whatever we serve you—good luck, fuckers.

We ate whole fried river crabs, cold soba, and Hida beef, all of which we loved. We also ate abalone for the first time, which, despite what Mark told me, still seems like it must have actually been an old sponge the chef scavenged from the trash can in the back alley and served to unsuspecting travelers.

Sometimes when the server brought the food she'd back away from us on her knees, bowing all the way. It started off being awkward, then we expected it, then we got offended when, at more modern restaurants, the staff would dare to turn their backs on us when they took our order to the kitchen.

In the middle of the trip Lisa and I got in an argument in the Kyoto train station, the kind where you're tired and hungry and don't even remember what it was about a day later, and an old Japanese man approached us and asked if he could help solve our problem. We think he just wanted to practice his

English with Americans. In Japan we got the feeling that asking a man, even an annoying one, who offered advice to please leave us alone would have insulted his ancestors going back a thousand years. So we listened to him for the next half hour as, standing in the middle of the station, he gave us his Ramen For The Soul advice on how much hard work a marriage is and how fighting doesn't make things easier. Then we got a Sapporo.

My favorite part of the trip was the time we spent in Magome and Tsumago, small post towns settled along the ancient road from Tokyo to Kyoto. Today the part of that road between the two towns is restored, and we hiked it. It took about six hours, and we saw bamboo forests, traditional water basins, and only three other people who each looked surprised to see us. Later on we met a local in Osaka who said she'd never even heard of anyone hiking that road.

Lisa enjoyed the hike in the way that she's glad to say she's done it, but I would do it again. I think it would be cool to hike the whole road if that's possible. Our vacations aren't on beaches or by pools, so we don't exactly relax while we travel, but out there between two little towns, away from the subways and metros and neon of urban Japan, I was serene, more so than when I was with my parents in the Poconos or skipping out to the woods for a long weekend with Mark.

When we decided to move, I thought it was to keep ourselves insulated, to reclaim the calm we had while we hiked on an ancient road, that we'd lost in Bella Vista. The back yard, the quiet—our house seemed like a refuge. But that wasn't it. The easy explanation never is.

15

THE WORKERS ARE GOING HOME

Sometimes I crave that bamboo forest feeling while I'm at work. During long Power Point presentations, waiting a half hour for a client to show up to a meeting, and, when I first got promoted to office manager, right before I had to fire someone.

I'm a little surprised my memories of the central Japanese woods have come back to me the last few times I've fired someone. For years it was just another calendar event, but not recently.

The first time I had to do it, I didn't sleep the night before. That morning I drank coffee for hours but couldn't bring myself to eat, so when I finally had to speak with her my hands were shaking, my stomach was partially corroded, and I couldn't focus my eyes on any one thing. In retrospect it all went as well as possible—she'd been underperforming, knew it, and so wasn't shocked when I told her. She quietly cleaned out her desk at the end of the day.

Now firing someone is like another meeting. Most of the time it's a kid from shipping who caused some trouble, and that's hardly a conversation. When it comes to letting go a salesman or accountant, I have my routine: It was the Sirs' decision, I'll write you a recommendation, and I see people get through this all the time. I don't see that, actually, but only because I don't follow up on people who no longer work for me.

When I told my father that it's best not to have an opinion in these situations, I didn't lie, but I also didn't tell him how easy that is. When someone gets fired they've either done something wrong or they're not making the company money, and if the Sirs want to get rid of someone that hurts their profits, I can't argue.

Except with Jim Walford.

I tried, I really tried to not care, to put myself back in the bamboo forest and soothe my anxiety, but he was our best salesman. If I told him he had to make up the losses we incurred from his mistake, he could have done it in six months.

But that's not what I do.

This morning I'm in my office on the phone with a lead. As I describe the merits of the saleswoman who covers the territory they fall into, someone raps hard on my door. This is not the soft knock of a salesman or delivery manager trying to figure out if my phone call is important or if I'm getting a grocery list for the evening. I hear the rapping again.

I ask the lead to please hold for just half a minute.

What? I ask when I open the door.

It's the office secretary.

I'm on the phone, I say.

Hattie Martineau for you.

Tell her I'll call her back.

No, Nathan, she's here.

Shit, I say. I have a pretty big potential client on hold, ask her if we can talk this afternoon.

She says she needs to see you as soon as possible.

All right, I say, tell her she can work in the conference room and I'll be there soon. Bring her coffee…whatever she wants.

Got it, she says.

I go back to the lead, apologize, and continue talking up the company and the potential sales rep. It takes half an hour, but I think they're hooked, and then I transfer them out to their very own Toaner Optic Networks agent, one who only has about forty-five other accounts.

Then I take the tie out of my desk, slip it over my shirt, smooth down my collar the best I can, and go get Hattie, the regional HR representative, from the conference room.

Hi Hattie, I say as I usher her back to my office, so sorry to make you wait, what can I do for you?

She makes sure I've closed my door behind us before she says anything.

There has been an undisclosed romantic relationship going on in this office, she says, for six months.

The hell, I say. Who?

Jillian Markov and Sebastian Shand.

Jill and Seb? I never would have seen that.

Apparently you didn't, she says.

Of course not. But, how did you know about it?

Stuart Cruman informed me last week.

He told you and he didn't tell me? Doesn't my HR person have to go through me and then you?

Not officially, Hattie says. Besides, he said he was sure you knew. I was told the situation was obvious and, at this point, untenable.

I did not know.

So you've told me.

And what do you mean untenable?

This is a clear breach of policy, she says. Both of them have to be terminated.

I can't fire both of them, I say. I just kicked Jill a huge

account a minute before you came in here. And Seb is the best IT guy on the East Coast. He once crawled into the ceiling and patched a wire with scotch tape to keep our systems running.

You'll replace them, she says. It's a rough economy out there, a lot of talent is looking for work.

At this point I lean back in my chair and exhale. Hattie doesn't move. She's sitting across the desk from me, a little angled on the chair, knees together, and even though I can't see them I'll bet her feet are together as well. Pumps pointed to the corner of the room. She has a folder with documentation of everything she's told me, but she's read it so thoroughly she hasn't needed to reference it while we've talked.

They've owned up to it, I say, right?

She says that they have.

So there's no problem, it's out in the open.

It wasn't for the last six months, she says, and we can't allow that sort of—

I know what we can't allow, I say, I've read every policy this company has. But if I fire Jill and Seb together, today, this office can't function.

You'll figure it out, she says, just like you did when you fired Jim Walford. Your branch's profits increased the next quarter.

Have you talked this over with the main office?

I work at the main office, she says. I did, however, mention it to the Vice President of Sales and the CFO, both of whom agreed with the decision completely.

And that's it. I'm good at what I do, but Hattie is a phenomenon. First of all, she's right, they did violate the policy. Secondly, Jill and Seb are fired already, and they probably know it. This is a matter of who tells them. And someone has to do it in a professional manner. Hell, Hattie could do that, the office secretary could do that. But after I do they'll respect the decision, the company. At least while they pack their things and leave the building.

Hattie gets up to leave.

I say, I'm sorry you had to come all the way down here. You could have called.

I was a little concerned that I hadn't heard from you, she says, so I wanted to do this in person. I also wanted to tell you that you ought to pay more attention to what goes on in your office. We should be doing this over the phone. OK?

Sure, I say.

You'll take care of it today?

Of course.

And she leaves. I close my door and take off my tie.

I don't want to fire them. I don't want my neighbors to think I'm a pedophile either, or for my wife to still be mad at me for doing something that would make everyone on our block think so, but here I am.

Before I call Jill and Seb into my office, I pull up my file of resumes. Hattie was right, there's plenty of talent, but like any other manager I like the known commodity.

This is how I wish I could handle it:

Jill and Seb come into my office and I begin with, I'm sorry to tell you this, but...Then I stop and sigh. I say, Fuck it. I pick up the phone, call the main office, and demand to talk to one of the Sirs. They say he's in a meeting but I tell them to get him out of the meeting, this is an important situation at the Bloomsbury County office. When he gets on the phone I say, This is Nathan Wavelsky and I know you've discussed the situation with Hattie Martineau but I will not be firing Jillian Markov and Sebastian Shand—they're essential to this office and, as far as I'm concerned, have earned a reprieve in this case. Then the Sir grumbles something about policy, but I insist that I will not terminate them. Finally the Sir tells me to hold, and I smile at Jill and Seb. Another Sir gets on the line and says, We're going to let you keep them, Nathan. We like the way you run an office and if you think they're necessary, that's fine, but if they screw up again, it's on you. Then I hang up the phone, tell them the good news, and remind them to live up to what I said about them.

But that's not what I do.

Jill and Seb come in my office late in the afternoon, stoical, and I say, I'm sorry to tell you this, but I have to let you both go. They nod, disappointed but accepting, and then I go through my routine. They look forward to hopefully using my letter on an interview in the near future, it's very generous of me to offer, and they're sure they'll make it somehow. They leave, they clean out their desks, everyone else notices but keeps working.

Both of them have taken their things out to their cars, and I thought they'd driven away, but then Seb walks back in through the front door. I see him weaving between desks on his way back to my office, and I start to wonder if he's the kind of guy who would have a shotgun in his back seat.

He walks into my office and gently shuts the door behind him, so the latch makes a small click to signal that it's closed.

Seb, I say, what's wrong?

He doesn't say anything as he walks towards me. He puts his palms on my desk and leans forward so his face is next to mine, close enough that I smell his cologne. And even though no one would hear us at normal volume, or be able to understand us through the walls unless we screamed, he whispers:

You fucking prick. You're supposed to stand up for your employees. For me, for Jill, for Jim Walford, after all we did to make you look good, to make your job easy.

Then he stands up and leaves. He walks through the office as if he'd just picked up a routine service ticket, and out the front door.

Everyone still at their desks, though, looks back at my office, so I get up and close my door, then slump back into my chair.

Your employees, he said.

My employees.

They're not my employees, someone else signs all our checks. I'm the parody of a cowboy the corporate world has created to watch its workers, make sure they move in the right direction, make sure the product fetches the right price at market. But all those big receipts go to the main office, not me.

During every review I've had at this company someone tells me that most people can't do what I do, which just makes me lose faith in most people.

On my drive home I think about sitting under white ash trees in the Poconos with my parents, about Mark and me driving to whatever spot in the woods we found and staying there for a few nights, about hiking through bamboo forests in Japan along an ancient route that even some of the natives don't know about.

And I think about Mt. Everest.

The way I picture it isn't the way it really is. When climbers show up at Base Camp in April there are surprisingly luxurious tents made of breathable nylon taffeta, hot food and tea, a medical staff, and available 3G wireless. Five hundred people are there, biding their time, waiting for a window in the weather. When that window comes, everyone tries to scurry up and, in the process, leaves their trash, which the Himalayan cold will preserve for generations.

Instead of all that I picture a snowy plateau miles long which ends at the foot of the mountains. I stand at the far end and look at the Himalayan range with Everest only the biggest of the massive peaks. I have a backpack full of freeze-dried chili and stew, a few sweets, Oolong tea, and a gas stove which I use to cook, brew, and melt snow for water.

It takes days to get to the foot of the mountains. There are no sounds but my boots crunching the snow, no colors but white and gray. I haven't seen another person since I started. Despite the cold I manage to write in my tattered Moleskine every night before I get a restless sleep in the frigid weather. The journal entries are always short. There's not a lot to record after a day out there.

Once on the mountain I climb at my own pace, camp wherever I find a suitable ledge. I spend a week crossing glaciers, climbing the ridges, and traversing the cols. When I'm close enough, I leave for the summit in the dark, around midnight, and get to it quickly. Then I sit in the little cap of snow for a few hours, munching on Romney's Kendal Mint Cakes like Edmund Hillary and Tenzing Norgay did, dangling my feet over the Himalayan range and the Tibetan plateau like I'm a kid sitting in a tree and looking down at my front lawn.

But that's fantasy.

When I get home and sit on my porch with some tea, I indulge that image for a little while longer.

16
AS COOL AS I AM

Mark is telling me about his new six month contract to help develop a boutique software firm's networking infrastructure. I don't really care. OK, I do care because he's my friend and I'm worried that he's taking on something he won't finish, but that's not what I want to talk about.

We're in this awful bar in Northeast Philly that he picked for reasons I can't fathom. The music is terrible. When Sweet Child O' Mine and We're Not Gonna Take It come on, the other patrons put their arms around each other, pump their fists in the air, and sing along. It smells like we got here the day before the weekly mopping. The light bulbs over the tables are of varying wattage.

I feel like there should be a fight club in the basement.

And I can get past it all because there's something I need to say.

Mark's going on about the idea he has for passive optical networks but I have no idea what any of it means. He does this because he's excited, that's all, and I really do want to listen, just not at this very moment.

Mark, I say.

No wait, he says, if you take this idea about attaining Brewster's angle—

Mark! I'm going with you.

Where?

Nepal.

Oh, he says, now you're accepting the invitation. Months later.

Yes, I say.

The glasses of beer in front of us each have a lukewarm sip left, and Mark's looking around the place for a waitress.

Well, he says while craning his head left and right, I'll have to have the guide come to meet you for a vetting, and we'll need to create a training regimen for you. I think you've gotten a little soft in the burbs, driving everywhere and not walking off your lunchtime hoagies, but maybe we can work something out.

You know I'll put in all the work, I say.

What? I know, I was just giving you shit.

He sees our waitress and yells, Excuse me! She turns, a little startled, and Mark orders refills of beer and two shots of whiskey.

I don't want to do shots, I say, I'm driving us home.

None of that, he says. My friend just agreed to come with me and climb the tallest mountain on Earth—we are drinking to this.

The waitress brings the shots before the beers, and Mark scoops his up immediately. I take my glass and raise it to his.

To the top, he says.

The top, I say.

And we put them back.

Mark lets his glass fall to the table with a knock. He looks invigorated by the drink. I hold my glass for a second while the burning in my throat peaks and dissipates. When the waitress comes over with the pints I ask her to please bring me a glass of ice water as well.

Now Mark's exuberant.

This is fantastic, he says. I would have done it alone, sure, but I'd rather stand up there together. And Lisa came around to the whole thing?

Right, I say, that's not exactly how it went down.

Oh. How did she react?

I'll tell you when she does.

You haven't talked to your wife about this?

No, I say.

Then I tell Mark about Rayanne, about loaning her the book, how her father came to my door, how angry Lisa got when the neighborhood started ignoring us, and how maybe now isn't the best time to talk to her about flying to Kathmandu and hanging out in the mountains for two months. This takes us through another beer.

Mark asks if Lisa's still angry.

Yeah, I say. She's hardly spoken to me at dinner over the past week, and she goes to bed early every night, just reads a book and doesn't look at me when I walk in the room or get in bed.

Sounds bad.

It is. It's like she has no idea what I was trying to do.

Which was what, exactly? he asks.

Loan a cool kid a cool book.

And give her music.

Yes, and give her music.

Come on, Nathan, that's not the relationship most adults have with the teenage girl next door.

What the fuck are you trying to say?

Nothing, he says, I'm not trying to say I don't believe you, I totally believe you. But I know you. They don't. And think about it from Lisa's perspective: here you are hanging out with a girl who's just like she was.

So what?

Like her when she was younger, with no wrinkles.

Lisa doesn't have any wrinkles.

Not that you see, Mark says, but she sees them.

Then Mark flags down the waitress and asks for two more beers. I interrupt and say that I don't want another, I'll just have a Coke.

You all right? Mark asks.

I'm driving you home.

I trust you with one more, he says.

I'm fine.

All right, he says. Anyway, Lisa sees herself in Rayanne but before time has been able to impart even minor imperfections. So she gets concerned.

You're saying my wife is worried I'm going to leave her for a teenager?

No, he says, your wife is concerned that you aren't committed enough to her. The teenager in concert t-shirts just exacerbates it.

The waitress brings our drinks, and Mark immediately takes two big gulps of his Yuengling. I take the useless stir straw out of my coke and sip it, letting an ice cube slip into my mouth. As it melts I feel a frigid creek trickle over my tongue.

So what is it? he says.

What's what?

What's making her doubt herself, and you?

I don't know.

Yes you do, he says. Or you're a shitty husband.

She wants kids, I say.

Of course she does, how is this an issue? You have good jobs, you bought a house with two more bedrooms than you need, and you've been playing music mentor to this kid who, I mean, if your kids don't turn out just like her I'll be shocked. If you don't have a kid, even I'll think you were leading your wife on.

We didn't talk about it until after we'd moved.

No excuse, he says. You're in it, and if you didn't see this coming I don't know what to tell you.

I drink some more soda and crunch a few ice cubes between my molars.

How did you get so wise about women? I ask.

I've been with a lot of them.

But not for more than a few months.

This is why, he says. When you really love a woman you don't see all this stuff, because you just want to love her. You don't see the imperfections and problems she sees, and the issues they cause, so when something comes up you—and every other husband—gets blindsided. You don't see Rayanne the way Lisa does, you just see a cool kid. You have to learn to think like her so you notice all that stuff. And it's hard, keeping that up. I see guys like you going through it and it's just not for me.

You seem like you'd be good at it, I say.

Yeah, maybe. Anyway, it's easier to fix someone else's problems than to see your own.

Well, I say, feel free to keep working on mine.

When you do tell her, he says, what are you going to say?

I have no idea. She doesn't want me to go.

Why do you want to?

I feel compelled to, I say.

Mark tells me that's not going to cut it.

I know.

Once you figure that out, he says, you will have to meet the guide. Ray, the guy I met on Denali, remember him?

Sure.

He'll be in New York for a while in February, and I'm sure he'll come down here to see us. You need to get on a routine before that, but I wouldn't worry about him taking you on. Once I give him your fee, he'll want you there.

I'll take care of that, I say.

The money? he says. Come on, Nathan, you just bought a house. And I asked you to do this. Really, I've got it.

No, I want to pay my own way.

That doesn't make any sense, he says. I can pay for it easily, and I know you can't. Let me do this for you.

Thanks, I say, but I'll get the money myself. I'll find it.

He concedes by finishing off his beer. He says, If you run into problems, the offer stands. OK?

Yeah, I say, thanks. The only thing I'm worried about is work. I don't know how to ask for eight weeks off. Speaking of that, what's with the new job? It's a little unusual to take on a project like that when you know you're leaving the country in April.

I was restless, he says.

Oh, training for this climb isn't enough for you?

No, he says. I was building this server for a guy who worked for me when I owned the company, and I couldn't think of any ways to improve it. Fully flash memory, super light aluminum case, the best processor available—there was nothing else to add. Until they come out with some new technology there's nothing else I can do to make the thing better. It drove me nuts. So I called a few people I know around here to see what they needed done and found this infrastructure project which I can definitely pull off before we leave.

To keep busy? I ask.

Basically, he says. To do something. Training's hard, but it's not like I was out of shape before. I don't look any different. At least with the job I see something new after every day.

Cool, I say.

I think so.

Are you sure you're not taking on too much?

I'm only ever worried about doing too little, he says. I can deal with losing sleep over work, I can't deal with the insomnia of boredom.

Then we get up to go. I'm tired, but sober. After I swing my coat over my shoulders I grab my glass and tilt a few Coke-stained ice cubes into my mouth before we leave.

As we walk over the cracked and crumbling blacktop to the car, I ask, Why do you like this place?

The people.

You're kidding, right? They're submentals.

Yeah, he says, but they're genuine. Go to a bar in Queen Village and watch the people. All they do is fake disaffection. Fucking hipsters. Nothing gets to them, nothing sparks a thought or feeling, they float above everything, they're too cool to experience the world. They heard about everything before it was popular and now they're over it. Fuck that. I'll take shit music and real reactions.

OK, but there's not a lot of conversations to have with the people in there.

Not when I'm with you. But otherwise I enjoy talking to whoever's next to me.

That sounds awful.

I know you think so, but I've made a lot of friends that way. Even just for the duration of a few beers.

If it makes you happy. I think I'd just be disappointed in what other people say.

That would make me feel a little closed off from the world.

Yeah, I say, it does. That's kind of what I'm going for.

You are the king introvert, Nathan.

Thank you.

When we climb into the car and I let it idle for a minute so we can get some heat, Mark punches me on the shoulder. Everest, he says, we're fucking crazy.

He falls asleep almost immediately after I pull onto the road. I play Vs. by Pearl Jam straight through, let the hard chords of Go and Animal keep me alert.

He's a genius, Mark. In his field, he could be a billionaire by now, but he's not into money. He's into making. There's no score in his life, no clock, there's just Am-I-Accomplishing-Right-Now. When I see the things he does, the taking on new jobs or the going to China, getting bored there, and then going off to Alaska…I'm glad I'm not a genius.

17
CONQUISTADOR OF THE USELESS

When you climb a mountain you accomplish nothing. The mountain, it's still there when you're done, and it doesn't care that you've scurried to its summit for a moment. You gain nothing tangible. You have not prevented someone from dying on that mountain the next season. You have no new insight into your soul, or the soul of the planet, or any other spiritual quasi-religious crap.

After you're done, you're in pain. And not the good kind. You are not in better shape for having climbed that mountain. When you summit you're using oxygen faster than you can take it in from the thin air. When you get down—if you get down—you may very well need medical attention. A doctor might have to put ointment on your cornea to combat snow blindness. Several of your digits may turn black with frostbite and have to be amputated.

There is nothing to bring back with you. You have not made a profit. You have, in fact, spent a great deal of money in order to do this, an investment which yields nothing except your having climbed a mountain.

You go up, you come down, nothing else.

And that is why I want to do it.

Expressing all that to my wife is difficult. Telling her, Hun I really really want to—that won't cut it. I'm not worried that she won't let me go, I'm worried that she won't want me to. If she understands, she'll want me to.

I've avoided this for too long, and now we're in our library, reading. It's so windy outside that we keep the window closed, which makes the room stuffier than we like. I've just brought fresh cups of Earl Grey tea for both of us when Lisa says, How's Mark?

This is good, I think, she hasn't started much conversation in the last week or so.

Fine, I say.

I mean, she says, how was your night out with him this week?

We had a good time.

You told me that when you came home and woke me up after rolling into bed. I want to know how Mark's doing.

Good, I say. He took a job with a company around here.

Really, she says. Isn't he still going to the Himalayas this spring?

He is, I say. He took a six month contract, so he'll be done before he has to leave.

Was he that bored?

He says so.

Wow, she says, I'd murder someone for six months off and then a two-month trip to Asia.

Yeah, I say.

So what exactly is he doing?

I don't know, I say, it's beyond me.

Didn't he tell you? she asks.

Yeah.

Well, what did he tell you?

Networking, I say, or something like that. I don't really understand it.

Don't you listen when your friends talk?

Sure, but that doesn't mean I get everything they say.

Fine, she says.

Then she picks up her book again, reaches for her mug, and takes a sip of tea. I look at my book but can't get through a sentence.

I say, I want to go with him.

She looks over at me and lets her book fall to her lap.

I know, she says. You told me that a while ago.

Yeah, but now I'm going to go with him. I told him when we were out the other night.

And when were you planning on talking to me about this?

Right now, I say.

Oh, she says, well then this might be a good time to tell you that I went off the pill two months ago and I'm ten days late.

Are you fucking serious?

No, she says, of course not, but that's about how dick you're being right now. What the hell are you thinking, not talking this over with me?

Oh, come on Lisa—

No, listen to me. Do you just want to live your own life or are we married? First you don't tell me about inviting teenage girls in the house, then you forget to mention that you're planning a trip to the Himalayas...What the fuck, Nathan?

That's not how I meant it.

Well, it's what you fucking did. This isn't even like a money thing, or a time thing, it's a risking your life thing. You don't get to go teeter over crevasses for two months without discussing it with me.

I know, you're right.

Why are you going to do this?

You know I had to fire two more people last week, and with the way Seb Shand reacted, it kept me thinking—

I know why you want to go, she says, but I asked why you're actually going to. I know why I want move to a villa in Tuscany and get five more cats, but I'm not going to do it.

Lisa gets up and leaves the room. Her tea is on the table next to mine, still letting out waves of steam. She goes to the bathroom and turns on the water, but I have no idea what she's really doing in there. Crying? Puking? I stop reading. My pulse is hard enough to vibrate my sweater. When she comes out I've finished half my tea, and she's patting her face with a towel.

Is this because you hate your job? she asks.

No, I say.

Really? Because you just mentioned that you had to fire more people and that it didn't go so well this time.

That's a part of it.

Did you ever wonder if the solution is to get a new job instead of going across the world to risk your life?

My job's fine, I say.

It's never what you wanted to do.

And you wanted to be a registration systems coordinator at a third tier university?

No, she says, but I'm not freaking out and leaving for some extreme adventure, saying, Bye Nathan, see you if I get back alive. You could do something you love, something you care about.

You sound like my parents, I say. I mean, if we're working jobs we hate, what would we like? Neither of us went to school for any practical training, or because we had some grand aspirations. We like books, cats, traveling, this library, Breeders concerts, Jeopardy. And philosophy classes, what about those? Don't you care about finishing that degree?

No, she says, and I never said I did. Just because they offered to let me have a degree doesn't mean I want it, but everyone else seems to think I do. And at least when I don't care about something it doesn't lead me to look like a pedophile, ostracize our neighbors, and climb a big rock on the other side of the planet.

It's not like that, I say. I may not give a shit about lots of things, like Congress, or the Pulitzer winners, or fancy restaurants, and yeah, I didn't show the best judgement when I let Rayanne in the house, but it wasn't because I didn't care. The things I care about, I care about them a lot.

And one of them is climbing a mountain.

Yes, I say, one of those things is taking this chance to climb Mt. Everest.

Fine, she says, I won't stop you.

Then Lisa walks out of the library and goes downstairs. I follow her, quickly, and wonder why I can't take stairs two at a time on the way down. Neither of us finish our tea.

I don't want you to let me go, I say as I walk into the kitchen just behind her, I want you to understand me.

You sound like a bitch, she says.

The hell?

You sound like me when I'm PMSing. It's not enough that I let you have what you want, you want me to know your feelings.

Yeah, I say, but this isn't like when you want to go to some overwrought chick flick. This is major, doing something like this helps define who you are.

If it is, then why can't you tell me why you're going to do it?

I fucking can if you'll let me.

Now would be a pretty good time, then.

Because nothing will ever be so simple again, I say. Nothing will ever be that focused and streamlined. Go to the mountain, get to the top, get down. It's not easy, but it's not complicated either. There's no ulterior motive, no race, no prize, no profit, no promotions—just me, getting to the top. It is wonderful and useless.

Lisa nods. She looks like she's trying to understand everything…or like she's thinking of how best to shake the sense back into me.

She asks, Why will nothing ever be that simple again?

Because we're going to have a family, I say. Kids don't really fall into that model of simplicity. I mean, look how much trouble I got us in for loaning someone else's kid a book, who knows what'll happen when they're mine.

Now you want to have kids? she asks.

No, I say. Well, not actively. But I've never met a guy who regretted it. None of them ever come in after their babies keep them up all night or their teenager gets detention and say, Man I wish I'd never knocked up my wife.

She doesn't say anything.

Sorry, I say, I don't want to lie about it, but maybe it's just that there's been nothing else for so long and I might be ready to make something else. I want to do this one more thing and then—

Shut up, Lisa says.

Are you going to cry? I ask.

No, just be quiet for a minute.

She grabs a glass from the cabinet behind her, fills it up with water and takes a gulp. Then she leans back against the counter.

She says, That is the most observant and introspective thing you have ever said. Now just shut up.

I'm a little stunned at this, but I do shut up. Lisa grabs a red dish towel for no discernible reason and starts wringing it even though it's dry. She looks like she's about to cry, but I haven't seen a tear yet. I look around for either of the cats, but they're nowhere to be found, which is just like them—absent when it would be so convenient to have them there.

Are you telling me that what I just told you is the smartest thing I've ever said?

She's still quiet, still clutching that red towel.

It was clever, I say, but I think I've come up with better ideas.

I didn't say it was your most brilliant moment, she tells me, just your most observant.

And introspective, I add.

Yes, she says. You said that you're like other people, and that you want to make something new. You never do that.

Sure I do.

No, you don't. You've spent a lot of energy distancing yourself from other people. You read, you listen to music, you put up these walls and have a strict gatekeeper. But now you want to let someone else in—because other people do.

Are we still talking about the mountain?

Yes, she says, kind of. I mean, the way you were with Rayanne, and now you're serious about having a baby...

Then she hops up and sits on the counter's edge. She leans forward, and I think this is when she's going to cry, but I'm wrong again.

Do you know, she says with a frustrated grin, that I've never worried about school? This master's degree, I never even think about it. It would be nice, but when I'm home with you, or out to dinner, even doing reading for a class, I never think about the degree. But then I see some baby while I'm driving and I break down uncontrollably. Then I try to redo our house by myself.

Not the best decision you've ever made.

That's the thing, it wasn't a decision. It wasn't a blank slate I wrote HOME-BABY-FAMILY on. It was a compulsive reaction. And I know what this Mt. Everest thing means to you, I really do, but I so don't want you to go and risk that part of our lives.

The baby.

Yes. The making a person that's like us.

I go over to her and run my fingertips through her hair and down her cheek.

She says, I really don't want you to go.

I told Mark I would.

That's not an excuse, Mark's not an adult.

Yes he is. He's a brilliant one.

Of course he's a genius, but he's not an adult. Not like we are, at least. He traipses around the world, takes six month contracts. He doesn't commit to things. And now you're acting like him, you want to put it all at risk for this trip.

And after that, I say, my attention's all back here. That's the end, once I do this I can move forward.

No, Nathan, this isn't going to make you into an adult like some rite of passage. You are an adult. It's already happened, past tense, done. You can't go back and be a kid for a few months now.

I don't see it that way.

Obviously, she says. I just, I thought we had it all figured out. We have each other and this house we love, and we were going to add a baby. But now there's this mountain in the way. They're bad enough when they're metaphors, a real one is serious shit.

This isn't a replacement for starting a family, I say. I still want that.

I believe you, she says, or at least I want to. But I still think that if you really wanted a family, if you did like I do, you wouldn't need to do something else first.

We have a quiet rest of the day so we can recover from that conversation. We read some more; she calls her sister (but does not, from what I overhear, tell her what we discussed); I find Tombstone on TV and watch it almost solely for the scene where Val Kilmer gets accused of being drunk and seeing double, then says, I've got two guns, one for each of ya. Lisa had bought food for dinner but once it gets dark she doesn't want to cook, so we order Chinese food. Our favorite place already knows what we want when I call, and they say, Half hour Mr. Wawewski! They are, actually, closer than almost anyone else to getting my last name right.

When we go to bed I try to read the last thirty pages of The Apprenticeship of Duddy Kravitz, which I'm a little shocked I've never read before, while Lisa watches some show about DIY home renovation. Before I finish I turn to her and ask, You're OK?

No. I don't know. Nothing's going to make me want you to go, Nathan, but I know you've already decided to. And, maybe I could like the idea that you have gone.

That's an interesting twisting of tenses.

I think you'll love going there, climbing, being with Mark, and I think you'll feel great about yourself when you get back. I'm just not sure it's worth it. I like you a lot right now, I don't know why you need something else, and I know that I don't need anything else.

Thanks, I say as I turn onto my side and kiss her cheek.

You do think you need this, that it's worth it?

Well, yeah.

Fuck, she says, then lets her head fall back on the pillow. I guess I need to trust you.

She reaches to the nightstand and picks up her phone, starts scrolling on it, through Facebook or Twitter or something like that.

I settle back against my pillows, read a few more pages, then turn back to Lisa.

How cool is that in a year or so I'll have climbed Mt. Everest and you'll be pregnant?

We hope, she says. And are you comparing climbing through the freezing cold at the cruising altitude of a 747...to pregnancy?

That wasn't quite what I meant.

After you come home and get around to putting a baby in me, I'm going to have to push a watermelon out my peach—don't disrespect childbearing again.

18
I'M WORKING, BUT I'M NOT WORKING FOR YOU

Hello Sirs, this is Nathan Wavelsky from the Bloomsbury County office. I'm calling to let you know that I will need to take ten weeks off, beginning with the last week of this coming March. It's because I'm going to the Himalayas to try and climb Mt. Everest. No Sirs, I don't really feel like I need to explain why I want to go. Suffice it to say that my office has been one of the top five most productive each year that I've been in charge, and that for the brief time I'll be gone, if we plan correctly, this place will be able to run smoothly without me. I will use my three weeks of paid vacation, but I do not expect that you will pay me for the other seven. If you feel that such action on my part warrants dismissal, I understand, but I believe that I have put enough quality effort into this company to earn this time off, which I assure you is for a unique experience.

That's how I sound in my car on the way to the office Monday morning—I'm articulate when I'm alone. I'll be at my desk by eight and call them before they've had time to read the emails which have been piling up all weekend. I think I sound pretty good. Confident. I'm wearing slacks and a tie today, even though I expect all of this to happen over the phone.

I actually get in at 8:02 because of traffic, and as I walk through the parking lot an email clicks through on my phone from one of the Sirs. It says to call as soon as I get in the office.

I'm the first one there, so I walk around and turn on all the lights. This time of year it's pretty dim early in the morning. Then I go to my office to switch on my computer, and while it goes through its network security routine I go to the break room and make coffee. I will not make this phone call without more caffeine, and the Starbucks on my way to work is off limits for a while after that run-in with Tom Harrison there.

Once the coffee brews and I have a steaming cup on my desk I call the Sirs. A secretary picks up.

Hi, I say, this is Nathan Wavelsky from the Bloomsbury office.

Oh, Nathan, she says, I'll put you right through.

That has never, ever happened. Even when they ask me to call I get put on hold while someone hunts down the Sir who requested me.

Hello Nathan, the Chief Executive Sir says a moment later. I'm putting you on speaker. Nearly the entire board is here with me.

That stuns me, it's never happened before, but with what I have to ask I don't want to show it.

I say, That's OK with me.

I hear the click and the slight hiss that comes when a whole room gets funneled through telephone lines.

Nathan, the same Sir continues, I'm not sure if you're aware of this, but Phillip Goddart resigned last week.

I was not aware of that, I say.

Phil has some health problems, he says, and had to leave the company in order to deal with them.

Oh, I say, will he be all right?

We don't know, but in any case the board of directors talked about this last week and we would like to offer you his position as regional coordinator.

I pause before saying anything because my mind is still on Phil Goddart, and when someone says health problems they mean something awful like colon cancer or Lou Gehrig's Disease. Phil was all right, a good coordinator, let me do my thing as long as it worked. Then I remember what I wanted to tell the Sirs in the first place.

Thank you, I say. All of you, thanks very much. This is a big surprise for me.

We thought it might be, one of them said.

So, will you take the position? another one asks.

Well, I say, there's a lot to think about. I'll have to talk to my wife about this before I can make a decision.

Regional coordinator is a step up for you in almost every aspect, the Chief Executive says. This offer won't last forever, Nathan. We need to have someone in this position right away.

Is it possible that you could give me some time? Phil traveled a lot, and while I'm sure the compensation is accurate, and that I can handle the responsibilities, I can't accept a lifestyle change of any sort without discussing it with my wife.

Someone else—the Senior VP Sir I think—says, We understand. How is Lisa doing?

I imagine their secretary looking up my file and scribbling LISA on a pad for the whole room to see.

She's great, I say. And I'm confident that she'll be as excited about this as I am, but I want a little while to discuss it with her.

How much time? they ask.

Three days, I say.

I hear some rustling on the other end of the line, but no one says anything. Can they communicate by nodding and straightening their ties? It wouldn't surprise me.

That's fine, they say.

Great.

So, we should expect to hear from you on Thursday morning?

If not before, I say, but there's actually one more thing I need to discuss with you.

Here is my advice to anyone in middle management: never ask for two and a half months off unless you're in traction. Or your daughter's just run off to Las Vegas with a talent agent and you need to track her down. Something like that. Not if you want to take a glorified hike with your college buddy.

Among all the mumbling and rustling on the other end of the phone, which sounds like a class full of kids who just found out they have a pop quiz, I hear them say, Disappointing. Outrageous. Unprofessional.

Despite their reactions, I interpret everything—the Sirs offering me a new job and wanting me to take on more responsibility—as a position of power. For me. They want me to do the job, so they'll do what's needed to get me to accept it.

Mr. Wavelsky, the Chief Executive Sir says, when we offer you a promotion, that is not a license for you to ask us for a favor in return.

I tell them I had planned on asking anyway, that I've already decided to go, and if that means losing my job I'm willing to pay that price.

I want to get into my prepared speech, but they don't want to listen.

Disrespectful, someone says. When we offer to put you in a new tax bracket, you tell us you don't want to come to work this spring.

Yes, I say, I understand how you could all feel a little taken aback by this. It's an unusual request to be sure—

An outrageous request, some other Sir says. You're supposed to set the example.

I believe that I have—

How could you maintain your authority if you're willing to abandon the company for months in a time of major transition?

I really don't think I'm abandoning—

Can we be sure you won't want to do this again in two to three years?

Well, to do this twice wouldn't be—

Nathan, this makes me seriously doubt whether you're the person for this position.

Fine, I say.

And I know right then that this thing I'm doing has been churning inside me for a long time, maybe since I was a kid—since I stood on my first peak in the Poconos, or read my first adventure book, or realized that I didn't give a shit about what everyone said I should.

For eight years, I say to the invisible office full of my bosses, I have set the example in this office. And you love it. This place runs like your kind of clockwork. Someone you want fired, I do it. Goals you want met, I meet them. You get so few complaints from customers about this office that when one came last year you thought it was a mistake. You want me in the coordinator job because you know I'll do the same thing there, but before I do that I want ten weeks off so I can get to the top of that rock.

I've never spoken to any of the Sirs like that before. This is what happens when for years you do what they say when they say, you do it well and you don't ask questions. You feel entitled to this moment of unloading everything inside you.

No one says anything for a few moments.

Then the Chief Executive says, You are not indispensable.

I know, I say, but I'll be pretty difficult to replace. If you think it's worth your time to find and train a replacement—two replacements really—I understand, but otherwise I think I've earned this time away.

They congregate again, this time for a little while longer. They don't ask me to hold. I hear some whispering, chairs getting rolled around, paper changing hands. They could have just told me they'd call me back. While this happens I see some people start to arrive. Jackson, the warehouse manager, Elaine, the office secretary. They see me through my office window and wave. I give a half-wave back.

OK, one of the Sirs says. Let us know the dates you would like to have off and we will find a way to work with it.

Thank you very much, I say.

After I hang up I stride to the bathroom, nodding to the people who are already at their desks. I grip the porcelain and stare at the drain. My spit is bitter. I think I'm going to dry heave.

Someone else walks in and sees me bent over the sink.

Nathan, he says, are you all right?

I look in the mirror and see that my skin is pale and my hair is all messed up.

Rough morning, I say. But I'll be fine, thanks.

~

Lisa is ecstatic about the job offer, except for one thing.

Where are we going to live? she asks. Isn't the main office in Connecticut? Won't they want you to be there a lot of the time?

That's a good point, I say, Phil was based up in North Jersey.

In a nice part of Jersey?

There are no nice parts of Jersey, I say. We're staying here.

Hun, it might be worth it to move.

We are not moving. I've barely unpacked and I'm never doing this again. I have my burial plot picked out under one of those spruces in the back yard.

So two days after they offer me the position I'm back on the phone, this time only with the Chief Executive Sir.

I would like to take the job, I say, but only if I can stay in Bloomsbury.

We would expect you to be in the Union County office, Nathan. We've bent significantly for you already.

You have, and I appreciate it, but my wife and I just got settled into our new house and we would like to stay here. I'm going to be traveling between offices for observations and meetings anyway, and as long as I have my cell phone there are about a half dozen ways to reach me.

He doesn't say anything.

And, I say, don't forget that you came to me with the job. You want me to do this. I would prefer staying in my current position over moving to the Union office.

I feel the bile pool under my tongue again. I think I've found the place where confidence makes me too big for my desk.

Fine, he says. Let me talk it over with everyone else. I think I can find a way for that to happen.

Thank you.

Do you have any other requests?

No, I say, this is it.

And I think to myself, Maybe don't push it again.

19
YOU MIGHT DIE

You might die, he says.

    I know, I say.

    Do you?

    Yes, I do.

    Do you?

    I understand that death is a possibility, I say, that it is not unlikely, that it lurks at ever so many turns.

    I'm at a bar with Ray, the guide Mark met on Denali and leader of the Peak Seekers Everest Expedition, which I am now a part of. Mark's late, but when I walked in I recognized Ray from the pictures on his semiprofessional website, which is really just a glorified blog. There's not a lot of time for web design in mountain ranges. We each have a glass of lager, but that's where the similarities end. Ray has the catcher's mitt leather skin and chicken wire beard you'd expect on a professional mountain guide. His blue fleece has a stain on the shoulder, like he spilled bleach on it. His voice sounds like cold air and cigarette smoke have shredded his larynx.

    I was in the Canadian Rockies last month, he says, climbing Mt. Robson. When I stopped on a ledge I looked across the valley and saw a team going up Resplendent Mountain, little dots in the distance against the snow. Then one of those specks started going the wrong way. Then that speck gained speed. I started counting, and it took that dot of a person thirty-seven seconds to fall to the base of the mountain. Thirty seven seconds of that person knowing they were going to die.

That's horrifying, I say. What happened?

I don't know. We never met up with that group.

Why did you tell me that?

Because, he says, you might die.

I get it, I say.

Do you? he asks. You're a novice. You did some hiking when you were younger, some hill walking in New England, and now you go camping once every few years. You're prime corpse material where we're going. Now, I'll take you because Mark says you'll be able to handle it, and Mark proved on Denali that he's got balls carved from granite, so I trust him, but you need to show me that you're more than a snack for a crevasse or dead weight on the end of our rope.

How do I do that?

Train, he says. Train hard. Train till your fingers are numb, your feet bleed, and you spit stomach acid through your front teeth. You've got three months to get in shape.

OK, I say, I'm in decent shape already.

Why do you think so, because you could beat your fat suburban neighbors in a foot race to the cooler of microbrews at the other end of the yard? None of that matters out there. You have to be tough, and tough up here, too.

Ray taps his temple when he says that. As he does, I wonder just what's rattling around in there.

Then Mark shows up.

Hi, he says, sorry I'm late. What are you talking about?

Training this guy, Ray says.

We talk for another hour while Mark and I each have one beer but Ray has three. He doesn't seem to change, though. He may have shown up drunk, or no longer feels the effects of alcohol. Neither would surprise me.

Mark and I agree, as Ray advises, to go to the gym four days a week, early in the morning. He tells us that it's the best time to go, not because it helps build more or harder muscle, but because it gets us used to exerting ourselves before dawn. He also tells us not to think that because we get all ripped that we're tough enough for the Himalayas, that avalanches don't care about how much you wailed on your lats or chiseled your quads, or how fast your best mile is on the treadmill. They'll eat you up either way.

I get it, I say.

Do you? Ray says back, then looks at me, unflinching, like the cold had paralyzed his face.

Yeah, I say, I get it.

I don't think I've ever set foot in a gym before lunch, but now Mark and I beat the morning rush to do leg presses, bench presses, squats, sit ups, and cardio on the elliptical, treadmill, and stair climber. The floor to ceiling windows are still dark mirrors when we arrive, and we only see the first orange light of cold mornings when we're done with our sets and walking to the showers.

It isn't long before those white rods of my arms start getting some muscle definition, and I feel pretty happy with myself.

Mark and I also go to an indoor climbing gym twice a week. It helps our technique, but mostly it's to keep the right set of muscles in shape. Lifting weights is great, but only climbing works exactly the right muscle groups, and even then we're not doing it in freezing temperatures, or at high altitude.

While I'm on these artificial walls that look like the surface of a Gaudí building and have holds that feel like a factory's parody of actual rock, I think about why I'm doing this:

Because there's some fundamental imprint on my brain after reading all those mountaineering stories as a kid? Because I freaked out when the neighborhood condemned me over the Rayanne thing and this is how I reacted? Because my friend's going and I'd otherwise feel like I'd missed out? Because this is my before-kids thing?

Probably some combination of all that which melds into an indistinct but powerful force and pushes me upwards, and which I'd otherwise have to resist my whole life. So I let it push, and hope I'm not wrong.

Over Presidents' Day Weekend, Mark and I take an extended camping trip to get our legs used to walking uphill. The Poconos aren't ideal for this sort of training, the ascents are too gradual and the altitude hardly taxes our ability to acclimatize, but with Mark's short contract and my new position we don't have the time to get out to the Rockies where we really ought to be. But February in the Poconos is at least cold.

The two of us have a small tent and the minimum of food in our backpacks. We're moving at dawn and asleep by nine, have no destination in mind, and push ourselves up as many of the rolling peaks as we can.

As we're on our way down from a summit one afternoon I say, The Himalayas will look like this in about 400 million years.

That's nice, he says.

You don't find that fascinating?

Not really, he says, in 400 million years we'll be dirt.

That's pretty morbid.

Sorry, he says, it's just that we have to focus. It takes concentration to get up a mountain.

I know.

On Denali my brain nearly shut down from the cold and the altitude. You can think about one thing: putting one foot in front of the other and not falling in the process. If your mind slips to that geology stuff, you're done.

Shit, I say, you sound like Ray.

Ray's crazy, Mark says, but he's right. You'll know it when you feel it up there. Just be ready, OK?

Yeah.

As we train, I also start my new job. My life doesn't change that much because of it. The pay raise is nice, and I can get myself a few shirts from Brooks Brothers instead of J. Crew. The biggest difference is that I spend more time in my car, visiting other offices around the region two or three days a week, which is made bearable, even enjoyable, by things like Weezer still making new music and Jay and Silent Bob having their own podcast.

I still have to semi-manage the Bloomsbury County office as we go through the process of hiring my successor. I'm involved in that, and it's a little surreal, hiring the new me.

I sit in on an interview with a candidate and Hattie Martineau, and the woman who applied keeps stressing her MBA courses. She took a class in operations management, one in HR, one in economics. She'd been working for ten years with Verizon, but only talks about her classes. I want to ask, What class taught you how to unjustly fire someone? Or how to do what you're told against your better judgment and still have the place make money?

We don't give her a second interview, but not because of that. Hattie takes her file to the main office, and in her cover letter and thank you email she used some fifty cent words one of the Sirs doesn't understand: My indefatigable work ethic… Thanks for choosing me for an interview out of the imbroglio of applications…The Sirs don't want to have to go to the dictionary in order to find out what's going on in Bloomsbury.

My training and new position allow Lisa and me to reintegrate into the neighborhood some. I'm never around. I can't get into more trouble at the gym or on the road.

And our neighbors soften their stances a little bit too.

In late February, when the stubborn patches of snow on the grass remind me every day that the weather isn't close to breaking, I pull into my driveway, jump out of the car, and run down to the mailbox before I go inside. I catch a glimpse of Alan Gillian walking to his front door. I stop and nod to him. He gives me a half wave back.

That's a win.

But the next morning I'm scraping ice off my windshield as my car warms up and I hear Alan call to me. He's walking across his frozen grass to my driveway.

Hi, I say.

Hi Nathan, he says.

We both shove our hands in our coat pockets. I'm not talking first, he came over to me.

I wanted to tell you, he says, that Rayanne's doing well.

OK, I say.

I mean in school. She's doing well, especially in English class.

I'm glad to hear it.

She did a report on Kurt Vonnegut, he says.

Really.

Yes, he says. She read a few more of his books, put together the report for her English class, and got an A on it.

I tell him that's great.

Yes, he says. She, well, she read them without my knowing, and I'd really rather she didn't do that. But if she's getting an A in something, it can't all be bad.

No, I guess not.

Anyway, he says, I thought you would want to know that.

I'm glad you told me, I say.

Then we shake hands, both of us with thick gloves on that thud together like pillows, and he walks back home.

The only problem I have before I leave is money. The fee to go with Ray's group is almost a quarter of what Lisa and I make in a year, which doesn't include my own climbing equipment and clothes, or my plane ticket. The new job helps us some, but I've only had it a few months.

Mark keeps offering to pay, or at least help out. We're in the middle of climbing an artificial rock wall at the indoor gym when he turns to me and says that he has his checkbook with him and could pay for everything right then. Or at least whatever I need.

Shit, I say, can we talk about this on the ground? What happened to that concentration on the mountain?

When we finish and are on our way to the locker room he says the same thing.

I don't want your money.

But I dragged you into this, he says.

You didn't drag me into anything. You brought it up, yeah, but I want to do this.

You know this is nothing for me financially, I just want to help you. I really want to.

That means a lot to me. It does, and that's one of the coolest things you've ever offered to do. But if I can't pay for this myself, I shouldn't go. That's just how I feel.

You sure? he says.

I'm fine, I say, don't worry about my bank account. If you really want to help someone, why don't you donate to one of those charities, the ones that help the families of climbers who died?

All right, he says, I can respect that.

Lisa and I get a little creative with money. We pretty much tap out our savings account, and we cash in a few of the mutual funds that our parents and grandparents started for us when we were kids—I doubt they saw us using it this way. We also cancel our IRA and 401k contributions for the four months leading up to the trip. We open up a new credit card for all the gear I need. We do the little things like packing our lunches each day and eating in on the weekends. That last one isn't hard for us.

This trip is not a financially sound endeavor. It's not safe physically, either. But we're never late on our mortgage or Visa payments, and I'm in the best shape of my life leading up to the day of my flight.

I actually feel a little like Mark: everything worked out for me. Things are better than when Lisa and I first moved.

And I still want to go.

That's how I know this isn't an escape or an excuse to get away for a few months and be my real self. I still don't know what to call it. A fulfillment? A compulsion? An adventure? It's a waste of time finding the right word, because none of it will matter if one unfortunate gust of wind blows while I'm traversing a ridge. It also won't matter if I bag the summit and come home unscathed.

20
KNOCK THE BASTARD OFF

Lisa drives me to the airport through an early spring rainfall. Usually it's twilight about now, but with the thick cloud cover it's already dark. The streetlamps and headlights reflect off the wet road, and I realize that the winter's snow and ice have shredded our windshield wipers.

We should get the wiper blades replaced, I say.

I should, she says. I should get them replaced while you're gone.

Yeah, I say.

I also need to take it in for state inspection, so I'll have them do it then.

Thanks, I appreciate that.

Right, she says.

That's about the extent of our conversation as we drive up the Jersey turnpike to Newark International.

Mark is having dinner with his parents tonight so he's going to meet me at the gate. I wonder if there would be less tension between Lisa and me if he rode with us.

Just as we see the Manhattan skyline in the distance, gray skyscrapers just a shade darker than the overcast, Lisa turns into the airport complex. She takes some of the bends around the terminals a little quickly for me. Drivers at airports are crazy anyway, but the rain makes it worse. I get the idea that if we got in a small accident and I fractured my leg and had to stay home, Lisa wouldn't feel all that bad.

I don't blame her. I can't wait to get that first glimpse of the Himalayan range, and to pick out Everest above all the other peaks, but I'm also panicked. It's not that I might die, which I might, it's that I might have to sit there for hours knowing I'm going to die. I read about one mountaineer who got near the summit of a mountain in the Caucasus when he lost sight in one eye. Instantly. The cold and altitude had popped his retina off. He knew he had to get down, but a few minutes later the other eye went dark too. His team couldn't carry him down, and he knew it, so he just sat down in the snow and waited to die. Which he did.

Maybe Ray got to me a little bit.

Someone else I read about fell into a crevasse in the Alps, not so deep that he couldn't be seen, but too deep for rescue attempts. They threw him a rope, but he was so tightly wedged in that even three guys couldn't pull him out. Eventually they knew it was hopeless, so he waited in the crevasse for hypothermia to take over, went numb, and died. The glacier swallowed his body over the coming days and weeks.

I don't fear the slipping, falling, or embolism deaths. I fear the abandoned and waiting for the cold to get you death. They happen every year in the mountains. I'm sure those people think about their families—I would have to think about the family I promised Lisa and couldn't follow through on.

Lisa parks in the short term lot. She takes in my carry-on while I lug my rucksack through the lines of cars, up the escalators, and to the check-in line.

Long line, I say.

Kathmandu's a hot place to go, she says.

We shuffle through the line, not talking much, dragging the bags by their straps across the linoleum floor each time we move up a few feet. I look at the other people and form little stories about why they're going half way around the world—the couple who can't stop laughing is going to a family wedding they think will be farcical, the kid in jeans and a long sleeved polo just lost his student visa and has to go home. Normally, Lisa and I would trade these little stories. But not tonight. Tonight we snake through the line quietly, checking our phones for the emails and texts we know haven't come through.

I get my boarding pass and send my backpack down the conveyor belt, and then all that's left is security.

Want to get a coffee? I ask Lisa. We're here in plenty of time.

No, she says, not really.

We get to the line, which isn't so bad, and I start digging for my passport which I just had when I checked in.

It's in your left jacket pocket, she says.

It is.

How did you know that? I ask.

I pay a lot of attention to the things you do.

Then we look at each other. I smile, because I think that's the sort of image I should leave my wife with before I go on this crazy trip.

Lisa says, Do you know how much I want to hit you?

What?

I want to lay you out, Nathan, so you have to look at your black eye every day and remember that you abandoned me, so the pain doesn't go away until you're about to land back here when you're done. At the same time I know what you're doing is incredible, and if you're going to do it I want you to get everything you can out of this. What does that mean?

I have no idea. But please don't deck me.

She puts her arms around my neck and squeezes. Then she squeezes pretty hard.

Lisa, hun, you're choking me.

She lets go and I see that she's crying.

I love you, she says. I want to smack you, and I love you.

I love you, too.

She says, I'm ready. I'm ready right now. For everything.

I think, I'm almost ready.

I say, I know.

We walk to the first TSA agent who takes my passport, shines a black light on it, looks at my boarding pass, and tells me to go ahead. I walk up to the line and start the slow march toward the scanners.

Hey Nathan!

I turn and see Lisa at the ropes.

Knock the bastard off, she says.

I take off my shoes and belt, empty my change into a bucket, pat my pockets to make sure I didn't forget anything, then go through the metal detector, which beeps. The agent takes me aside, has me spread my arms and legs apart, puts on his blue latex gloves, and starts the pat down. I know he doesn't enjoy this anymore than I do. My instinct is to turn to Lisa and mouth something lewd or let my eyes roll back.

But she's on her way back to the car.

Probably just as well, as she'd yell at me for risking getting arrested over something that's not too funny.

I get through the pat down with no problems, get

dressed again, and go to the gate where I pull out the box of Cheez-Its I brought for the flight. By the time Mark shows up I've finished about half of it.

He bounces up to me with his arms out, like he expects me to pop out of my seat and hug him. I remain sitting.

You're kidding me, he says. In an hour we're going to be on our way to Nepal and you're slumped in an airport chair, shoveling Cheez-Its into your face by the handful. You look like you're stress eating.

Yeah, I say.

Anyone else would think you're going home to see your dog one last time before he gets put down. What's the matter with you?

I tell him I'm just thinking about what we're doing.

You've had six months to think about it, he says. What hasn't processed?

It's different when you actually do it. When you leave your cats, hug your wife for the last time, and hand the guy your ticket.

It's exciting, he says.

And nerve wracking, I say.

He sits down next to me and reaches into my box of crackers.

Relax, he says. We're going to knock the bastard off.

Why do people keep saying that?

That's what Hillary said when he came back from the summit in '53: Well, George, we knocked the bastard off.

Who was George?

Another guy on the team, Mark says.

Wow, I never knew that.

That's a little surprising, he says.

It is.

So, what are you worried about.

Lisa, I say.

She'll be fine.

I tell him that I'm not worried about her making it through three months.

Oh, Mark says. I'm a little worried about that too. With my parents and all. It's not the same, but still.

How was your dinner with them?

Fine, he says. My mom got all weepy and my dad squeezed my hand extra hard.

They're worried, I say. This is dangerous.

They did the same thing when I went to China, he says, and to college for that matter. Any time I go beyond a certain radius of the house where I grew up they act like I'm never coming back.

You sure you're not Jewish?

Catholics aren't so different, he says. How did your parents react?

They see the whole thing as spiritual, I say. Lisa and I had dinner with them last night and they kept telling me to have fun and open myself up to the whole experience. I didn't know how to tell them that climbing, it's not fun, and there's no mystical crap involved. That there's no bigger reason for it.

Mark asks, Why didn't you just say that?

They just seemed so proud of me, like they never have before. They said things like I'll learn so much about myself, and I can do anything when I put my mind to it.

What's wrong with that?

I don't look at this as self discovery. Do you?

Everything's self discovery, he says.

This isn't quite such a Sartre thing for me.

What?

Sartre said people are constantly becoming.

That's kind of cool, he says. And, they are.

I'm about ready to stick with the way I am.

That sounds nice, he says.

It's not bad, I tell him.

Well, the way you are is all right. Cut your parents a break, they did a good job.

I know. I just don't think a parent's job is to tell their kids how to experience something. That's pretty individualistic.

Look at you and your parenting philosophy. Come around to Lisa's way of thinking?

I don't think hauling up the Himalayas portends good fatherhood.

All right, however you want to look at it. Then he gets up and says, Hold on a sec. He walks over to the desk in front of the gate and talks to the airline staff there. At one point he points back at me. Then he walks back over and says, Go up to the counter. I got us seats together.

OK, I say, and then walk to the same desk where they take my ticket and reissue me one for first class. I tell them I can't afford an upgrade and to put me back in my original seat, but they say that the other gentleman had paid for it. I look back and Mark smiles.

When I get my new boarding pass and sit next to him he says, I can treat you to this, right?

Yeah, I say, I wasn't expecting much luxury on this trip.

You won't get much, he says. You shouldn't. Going places in private cars, staying on the thirtieth floor of five-star hotels—you miss the authenticity.

But not flying coach?

Nothing authentic about being packed in at the back of the plane, he says.

We then take turns watching the bags while the other gets food as we wait for the plane which is, of course, about an hour late. Mark has two Whoppers and a milkshake and I go to a deli where I get a turkey sandwich that is somehow soggy and stale at the same time. Then Mark breaks out a Hershey's bar.

Want one? he asks.

No, thanks. Are you just going to demolish all the training we did during one hour in an airport terminal?

This is the last American food we're going to have for a while. Enjoy.

OK, I say. Give me that Hershey's bar.

The big difference between first class and coach is whether your vacation starts when you get on the plane or off it, and since this trip doesn't involve much relaxation, a chair that folds all the way back into a bed is a pretty nice final creature comfort.

We've been flying for about an hour and a half when Mark leans over and asks me what I'm reading. The flight attendants have just cleared our dinner trays and the people in the seats across the aisle have blankets over them and their eyes closed. We have to whisper.

The Innocents Abroad, I say. I have Death Comes for the Archbishop in my bag.

Why? he says.

Because they're good, I say.

Don't you want to get in the mood for climbing? I brought The Snow Leopard and The Climb if you want either of them.

No thanks, I say. I read The Snow Leopard, and I'm not into the whole Buddhist thing. What's the other one?

Anatoli Boukreev's story of the 1996 Everest disaster, he says.

I think I'll take a pass on reading about the deaths that have happened where we're going.

I've got a National Geographic too, if you want it.

I'm fine with what I've got.

OK, he says. You just seem a little detached is all. You remember how cool all this is, right?

Yeah. Don't worry about me. Besides, I hate reading about where I'm going before I get there. I almost never crack my Lonely Planet book until I'm on the final descent.

I'm sure Lisa loves that about you.

She doesn't care, she's the planner. If we were born thirty years earlier she would have started her own travel agency after college. She buys three or four guide books, registers for every online forum, and she's got days mapped out hour-by-hour sometimes before we go. It's amazing.

So you get to just show up for vacations, he says.

We're the perfect pair, I say.

Mark nods a little. He then torques his neck in both directions until it cracks.

You're all right, though? he asks.

I'm fine, I say. When we land in Kathmandu, you'll see.

21
THE MONKEY TEMPLE AND RUM DOODLE

Kathmandu stinks.

In Philadelphia, small patches of the city reek like open sewers all the time. We call them stink pockets. The southwest corner of 10th and South, across from the Whole Foods, smells like a toilet's been backing up there for days. These are all over town, all year long, and the rest of Philly has a general background smell of nondescript city grime.

But Kathmandu is a different level. It has a temperate climate, industrial technology from about the 1950s, and it's in a valley—all of which basically make it a bowl of pollution. Whatever particulates of smog and filth are the air, they make their way to your tongue and stick in between your taste buds.

If you're outside a lot, you have to protect yourself from it.

In Tokyo I saw people wearing surgical masks. They felt sick, and the masks were their way of being courteous and trying not to spread germs.

In Kathmandu policemen wear those masks all the time just because they have to be on the streets for a full shift and breathe in the polluted air.

It's actually worse at night because of the way air circulates around the valley—the bad air leaves the city, hits the hills, and comes back after sundown. Fortunately, when

Mark and I arrived last night we were so tired from twenty hours of traveling, even in plush chairs with free liquor, that we could have fallen asleep strapped to the top of a coal plant's smokestack.

Today, our first full one in Kathmandu, is our only free day. Beginning tomorrow we'll be meeting with Ray and the rest of the group for two days, then we leave for Base Camp.

I meet Mark in the lobby of our hotel before breakfast.

He asks, How'd you sleep?

Fine, I say. You?

All right, he says.

We decide to eat at the hotel because it's easy, has seemingly safe food, and does not require us to go outside. They serve us Roti—unleavened bread, like matzah without the perforation—and potato curry, which is a little spicy for breakfast. I think that it would taste great in about five hours. We only drink bottled water, though I imagine there's a possibility that it's bottled from the taps we're trying to avoid. They don't serve coffee, only chai tea, which has to do.

Mark says, We don't have time to explore the city, so I think we should pick one place to go today and otherwise take it easy.

That'll work. Do you have anything in mind?

The Monkey Temple, he says.

What?

It's a Buddhist temple on the outskirts of the city, and hundreds of monkeys live there. It's supposed to be amazing.

The outskirts, I say. Sounds good to me, I feel like I'd need days just to get adjusted to the air in this place.

I know, he says. There's a bus in two hours and we can get there by lunchtime.

Perfect, I say.

~

The bus is full of western tourists, and the driver makes announcements in broken English. So broken that I don't understand most of what he says, so I read through my guidebook's entry on the Monkey Temple, which makes me a bit car sick. I also look out at the neighborhoods we pass through. I hear the other people on the bus call the places quaint or authentic, but they look impoverished to me. The facades of the apartment complexes are crumbling, and the vendors on the side of the streets operate under tarps hung across four wooden stakes. There are no sidewalks, just dirt and patches of weeds between the road and the buildings.

I wonder whether the people who live in these homes would trade their authenticity for a Brita and a microwave.

When the bus arrives all I see are some statues of Buddha, and the start of a flight of stairs. My guidebook says it's 365 steps to the top and the stupa, the dome with the sacred relics. Mark looks up and says, Let's go.

I say, Aren't we going to climb enough while we're here?

We've got one day in this city, he says, we should do this right.

And we start the ascent. That we're winded by the time we get to the top doesn't instill confidence in me that we'll make it to the real summit.

The stupa is a white dome with a conical stone tower emerging from its center. There are two eyes painted on the tower, the all seeing eyes of Buddha. They're purple, and look a little sinister, like an Old Testament Buddha.

Mark starts meandering around the complex, where

there are stalls selling postcards and Buddhist souvenirs, along with the religious prayer wheels and incense. I find a bench. I take out my Mark Twain and start reading it, but after a page I notice the monkeys. Little brown ones with red faces. They don't get close, or at least close enough to touch, but you can always tell they're there. Watching you. They're a little like my cats, and not much bigger, except they probably have rabies.

When Mark finds me I'm on one end of the bench, trying to get through a chapter, and a monkey's on the other end.

He says, You made a friend.

Then the monkey hops off.

Not really, I say.

You should see the view of the valley, he says.

I put the book in my bag and we walk over to the observation point, where we get a view of the entire Kathmandu valley. Since the city doesn't have much of a skyline, we see the whole of it and the hills in the distance. And the smog cloud over it all.

This place is a dump, I say.

Since when did you become a xenophobe?

I'm not, I'm just not here for cultural exploration.

Maybe you could use a little Buddhism in your life, he says, a little Zen. It'll calm you down, let you see what's around you, in the moment.

I do want that, I say, but I'm not into Buddhism. When Lisa and I stayed in a Buddhist temple in Japan, I thought it was too beautiful and well kept a building for a group of people whose fundamental religious tenet is to eliminate desire. They were also anxious to sell us beers for a thousand yen each.

What about here, Mark says, on a hill, overlooking everything, removed from the city, just like you want to be.

The monkeys come from lice, I say.

They have lice?

No, I say, they come from lice. I read the mythology
of the place in my guidebook. A Bodhisattva—of wisdom I
think—raised this hill and was supposed to keep his hair short
while he did it, but he let it grow. So it got lice. And the lice
turned into the monkeys, who are sacred. Because they come
from the lice of the unkempt head of a prophet.

That's kind of gross, he says.

I think so, I say.

We look out at the valley for another few minutes.

It is a nice view, I say, but I can't get into sacred lice
monkeys. I don't like Buddhism, I just like the quiet.

When we get back to the hotel Mark wants to walk around,
find a late lunch, but I just want to lie down in my room. On
my bed, I stare at the ceiling and listen to my iPod on shuffle.
I don't sleep, but I drift, and occasionally get jolted awake
by the opening chords of a Replacements or Superchunk
single. I think that one day I'll have to come back and travel
through Nepal properly, but now I'm focused on getting to the
mountains, on seeing Everest and getting to the top.

And getting home.

As I get ready to meet Mark downstairs before dinner I
look out my window at the street, and keep my headphones in.
Devil's Haircut comes on. I see women in saris walking in the
middle of the street, compact cars that look like they've gone
over two hundred thousand miles weaving around them, a group
of military police officers, and the stalls closing up for the day.

My music—the angst of suburban kids who didn't fit in,
captured in three minute cuts—doesn't belong here. Neither

do I. Not right now. I like the situation that way, it keeps me focused on what I'm here to do.

Mark and I meet in the lobby again before dinner, and we walk to The Rum Doodle. It's a famous mountaineering bar where almost everyone on their way to Everest has a drink or ten before leaving Kathmandu. When we walk into the place we see that the walls and rafters have paper Yeti feet on them. Each of the feet has names, stories, poems, profanity, even songs scribbled on them from mountain travelers who hit the bar along their way.

We get a table, order beers, and look at the menu.

Marks says, What's with the food here?

Lots of chicken on the menu, I say. Even pizza. I can do with that.

It's tourist food, Mark says.

It is, I say, but I'm less than a tourist on this trip. I'm here for one reason.

Come on, he says, lighten up tonight.

Weren't you telling me before we left that if I let my concentration slip for a minute I could die?

Yeah, he says, on a mountain. We're in a bar.

I'm practicing.

The waiter brings us our beers and I order barbecue chicken. Mark orders pasta.

I say, Maybe we would like this better after we've been hiking, camping, and climbing for five weeks.

Probably, Mark says.

We look around at all the paper feet and try to read them. A lot are in English, but plenty are in another language. Mark points at one and says, What's that written in?

Welsh I think. There are a lot of Ys. The one behind your head says Abandon All Hope.

I picked the wrong table, he says. The one on that wall says Knocked The Bastard Off.

How did I never know that? I say.

We're done with our first beers by the time the food comes, and we eat quietly. The bar we're in is named after a book parodying mountain climbing—in the story, Rum Doodle is the tallest mountain in the world at 40,000 and ½ feet, and a group of bumbling but lovable climbers try to summit it.

I feel a little like them. Except less lovable.

The tallest mountain I've ever climbed was about five thousand feet. Everest is twenty nine thousand. Climbing tourists like me were a major cause of the 1996 disaster which killed eight people. We clog up the mountain. Get stuck where instincts (which we don't have) and technical skills (which we never practiced) should take over.

What happens on Everest this year will be a parody of what Hillary and Messner did.

But it's still the mountain. It's still summiting.

Mark and I get pretty drunk at Rum Doodle. Patrons arrive in groups and yell in various languages, sometimes buying shots for citizens of their country. When some Americans come in Mark goes over to them and talks his way into a few rounds of whiskey. I take one shot with them, but lay off after that. I sit on the edge of the group while they and Mark trade stories.

Sometime during my last beer of the evening I see a box behind the counter with a pile of papers in it. It looks like something for a raffle. I walk up to the bartender and ask what's in it.

That's the Everest club, he says in excellent English. We have the signatures of almost everyone who's ever climbed the mountain in that box. Even Edmund Hillary and Tenzing Norgay.

That's pretty cool, I say.

Are you going there? he asks.

Yeah, I say.

Maybe you'll put your name in later, then.

Hell yes, I say.

Then I gulp down the rest of my beer and find Mark. We have an early meeting with Ray.

22
PANIC

I'm in the hotel lobby alone the next morning and sitting on a large chair with seven or eight throw pillows on it, enough that I'm basically on the edge. It must be decorative. Mark hasn't come down yet, so I'm watching the other guests leave the stairwell and walk out to do whatever they came here for, always thinking the next one should be him. I wait like this for about ten minutes before I go up to his room. We have to meet everyone else on Peak Seekers at Ray's hotel, a short walk away, in twenty minutes.

I jog up the stairs, turn the corner into his hallway, and then knock on his door.

No answer.

I knock again and yell for him.

I hear, Come in. His voice is muted, like he yelled through five walls.

When I walk in I find that's not far from the truth. He's in the bathroom with the door shut. I hear him coughing.

We've got to go, I say, time to suck it up. Your hangover can't be that bad.

He says nothing, so I open the bathroom door.

Oh fuck, I say as I turn around and gag. Mark's been puking for a long time in that little bathroom, and I just unleashed the stench of it into the main room, and probably the whole hallway. I open the window and crack the door to try and get a cross breeze. I'll take the pollution over this.

What happened? I ask.

I don't know, he says, I just got up this morning and started barfing.

Then he does it again. A chunk splashes out of the toilet and gets stuck on the side of the bowl. This is more than a hangover. I start to feel pretty sick too, and I'm thankful that Mark has short hair.

What are we going to do? I say.

I'll be fine, he says and pushes himself up on his knees. I'll be fine, just give me a few minutes.

You might be fine in a few days, I say, but not today.

No, he says, this is when you have to toughen up.

Then he tries to stand, can't, falls, and hits his head on the side of the toilet. Now there's blood and puke on the porcelain. I hold down my own stomach acid as I pull him out of the bathroom and call for help.

Ray comes into the hospital waiting room around lunchtime and finds me paging through some magazines.

Any of those in English? he asks.

No, I say, but at this point I'm ready to teach myself Nepali.

You missed the meeting this morning, he says, it was important.

You don't fucking say, I tell him. I've been a little busy for the last few hours, but maybe I can make up the work after school.

We'll talk about it over a beer tonight, he says.

I don't give a shit, I say, I'm trying to find out whether or not my best friend is alive or dead.

You think he might be dead?

No, I don't actually think he's dead, but I can't get any information out of the people here. The doctor barely speaks English, and the nurses don't at all.

Ray asks what exactly the doctor said.

Nothing enlightening, I say. Very very sick. No shit, we're in a hospital.

A few minutes later I see the doctor walking past the nurses' desk and I run over to him.

Excuse me Doctor, I say, can you tell me anything else about my friend?

Friend? he says.

Yes, I say. Um, American. Sick American.

I catch myself speaking loudly and slowly, like that'll help him understand the language.

Oh, he says, very sick.

Will he be better soon?

The doctor just looks at me.

I say, Doesn't anyone here fucking speak English?

Frustration makes everyone regress a little bit. Or a lot. This is what I tell myself as the doctor scowls at me and walks into another patient's room, and the nurses avert their eyes when I look over to them.

Ray taps me on the shoulder.

Go sit down, he says.

I do, and from my seat I see him talking to a nurse at the desk, smiling, like he's flirting with her. A minute later he sits next to me and says someone else will be down to help us soon.

Did they teach you Nepali in New Zealand public school? I ask.

No, he says, but I've been here before, and one of the

only things you need to know is how to ask if anyone in the building speaks English.

Oh.

But, in New Zealand they do teach us how to ask politely.

Sorry, I say.

It's fine, he says, I'm almost glad this happened.

Why?

Because now it's out of you, or it better be.

What?

Panic, he says. Don't panic on the mountain.

The hospital director, the only employee in the building who speaks fluent English, comes to talk to us about Mark. He's wearing a three piece suit with a gold watch chain arcing along the vest, and looks like he misses the British Raj. He offers his hand to each of us, smiles, and apologizes that no one else could help.

How is Mark? I ask.

Your friend has a nasty virus, he says, and is now quite dehydrated. Fortunately that is all, and he should be fine in a week. You can even take him back to his hotel today.

What about his head? I ask.

Just a bump, he says, nothing serious at all.

We're leaving in two days, Ray says, will Mark be able to come with us?

To the mountains? the director says.

Everest Base Camp, Ray tells him.

Are you hiking the whole way?

No, Ray says, we're flying to Lukla.

Mark would probably make it, the director says, but if

you're taking a small plane there's a very good chance someone else will catch the virus. I frequently see it in tourists.

So we should leave him here, Ray says.

I'm afraid that if someone came down with this virus and couldn't rest comfortably for several days, they would be in real danger. With vomiting like you've seen in Mark one loses fluids quickly, and it would be difficult to replenish them properly while on such a journey. I know that you must have limited supplies along the way.

And we can't stop for someone, Ray adds.

Of course, the director says. My advice would be for you to keep him away from your team until he feels completely recovered. These viruses spread easily in close quarters.

Thank you, doctor, Ray says.

Yeah, I say, thanks.

We both shake his hand, and he leads us to Mark's room so that we can take him back to the hotel.

Mark takes the news with a stoicism and resignation that surprises me. Back in his hotel room he crumbles onto the bed, almost in the fetal position, and says, I'll catch up with you.

OK, I say. Just make sure you get better, then worry about following us.

I'll think of a way to get there.

Maybe just go to sleep now, I tell him.

I hear him snoring a little by the time I click the door shut behind me.

Walking back to my room I think about going home and taking Mark with me, but then I realize this is nothing but bad luck. He got a virus, he'll be OK.

From my bed I dial the twenty or so numbers it takes to

get through to America and call Lisa in her office to tell her about Mark.

Shit, she says, what are you going to do?

I'm going to keep with it, I say. I can't bail on this because my friend got the Nepalese flu.

Will he be able to catch up with you? Lisa asks.

I don't know, but if he doesn't I'll still keep going.

Does Mark want you to? she asks.

Mark wants to go to the meeting tomorrow morning and just bring a bucket to keep next to his chair.

OK, she says.

That's her OK of disapproval, I'd catch the tone over any phone line in the world.

I say, I'll be fine.

I know you will.

She doesn't mean that.

When we're done talking I take out one of the granola bars I brought with me and eat it while I find a way to prop up my iPod and watch a South Park episode. I loaded about thirty of them on there before I left. I'm still a little jet lagged, though, and I fall asleep for the night before it's over.

The next morning I'm in a meeting with the expedition team in a room at Ray's hotel. There are nine clients without Mark, and then Ray, the leader. We'll meet our Sherpa guides at Lukla in a few days.

Ray tells us that since we now understand the logistics—which he went over yesterday while I was at the hospital with Mark—we have to discuss safety. The refrain of You Die shapes his speech. It's like the first time I met him.

Broken leg, Ray says, and you die. AMS and you die. Snow blind, none of us are carrying you down, so you die.

I've heard a lot of this before.

Then he tells us about all the little things which can kill you where we're going. Someone on last year's expedition walked out of his tent at 6,200 meters to take a piss, didn't put on his crampons, slipped, and fell into a crevasse. They never found him. Somewhere inside Everest is a frozen man who didn't even get to put his dick away.

Base Camp, he says, is at a higher altitude than any place in the continental United States. It's higher than Mont Blanc. That makes all of you amateurs as soon as we get there. But people like you summit on my teams every year because they've done what I told them to. The people who don't get an obit in their local paper back home.

Ray goes on for almost an hour, but no one even looks scared. As I sneak glances of each team member I start thinking that I'm the youngest one in the room. I know Ray's in his mid-forties, but everyone else looks like they could have teenage kids at home too. Maybe they're just more experienced climbers than me, and years of high altitude winds haven't been kind to their skin.

As it turns out, both are true.

I speak to a few people when we break for lunch and each of them has experience on bigger and tougher mountains than I do. One guy has climbed all of the 14ers in Colorado—the 53 peaks above 14,000 feet. A woman from New Mexico, my age, has won three vertical free climbing contests, all without safety ropes. A Scottish guy has climbed Mont Blanc and the Matterhorn twice each.

I've walked up a hill in Maine.

This trip is everyone's first in the Himalayas, which is a nice common ground, but I am afraid of being dragged along, of holding everyone else back.

After the meeting, which involves lectures on properly using an ice axe to self-arrest and belaying in the case of an emergency, I go right back to my hotel and check on Mark, who's sound asleep, but has empty bottles of juice and water on his nightstand, which I take as a good sign. I go to my room and lie down. I want to ignore Kathmandu, to eliminate distractions, to focus on the mountain. Even here, in this city so foreign you could fit most of it in a fantasy novel, I have no interest in anything but the summit of a particular peak. I put on my iPod and listen to some Throwing Muses tracks, play Counting Backwards and Not Too Soon over and over.

Tanya Donelly sings, You might as well be dead if you're afraid to fall.

But that band writes some pretty surreal lyrics.

Eventually I fall asleep, a fitful one where I wake up often, each time just long enough to know that I'm awake, which ruins my rest.

23
LUKLA, NAMCHE BAZAAR, DINGBOCHE

The following morning we're leaving for Lukla. I take my bags down to the lobby, and have a porter watch them while I run up to Mark's room before the van with the rest of the expedition picks me up to take me to the airport. Mark hears me as I crack his door open and he rolls over. I stay in the doorway.

He says, I haven't puked in almost a day.

That's a good sign, I tell him. I'm leaving in a few minutes, just wanted to say good bye.

I'll see you soon.

You think you'll find a way to meet up with us?

You want a toe, he says, I'll get you a toe. With nail polish.

When he's quoting Coen Brothers movies, I know he's going to be fine.

Cool, I say, just take care of yourself. Don't leave until you're a hundred percent.

I'll catch up with you, don't worry.

I won't, I say.

Then I shut his door and run back downstairs.

The van comes a few minutes later. It is of an indeterminate make and model. The best I can describe it is a cross between a VW Bus and a Jeep Cherokee—not quite a full van, but bigger than an SUV, with a white roof, chipped blue paint, and a rusted grille.

Ray and the rest of the expedition are already in there. The hotel porters help me shove my bags on top of everyone else's, and then I climb into the van, onto the back bench. It has no seatbelts, but since there are five of us squeezed into seats made for three people we might not move at all in an accident.

At the airport we unload our things, check in, and wait in the terminal for our plane. While I'm sitting there, still reading Twain, a kid sits down next to me. He drops his bag between his feet, leans back and puts in his white earbuds. This kid looks like he's still in college, but he wears his North Face and Timberland gear like it was custom-tailored for him. His blonde hair is parted on the side and somehow looks classic and cool at the same time. He's got posture so good you notice when you walk by.

After a minute he takes out one of his earphones and asks me if I'm waiting for the Lukla flight.

Yeah, I say.

It's at this gate?

Yeah.

Thanks, he says and then puts his earphone back in.

Ray walks by us a little later and taps the kid on the shoulder.

I've got it all worked out, Ray says, nothing to worry about.

The kid says, Thanks.

Then Ray keeps walking and I jump out of my chair and catch up with him.

Hey, I say, who is that guy?

That's Marshall, Ray says, he's taking Mark's seat on the flight.

So, he's just going to Lukla?

He's coming with us to Base Camp.

He's taking Mark's place on the expedition, then?

Marshall's not climbing, Ray says, he just wants to see the mountains.

We don't have enough room in the tents. When Mark catches up with us where will we put Marshall?

If Mark catches up. And if he does, we'll figure it out.

Come on, I say, Mark didn't bail, he got sick, and he'll catch up with us somehow. You have to keep his spot open.

At this point Ray loses all signs of good humor. His eyes narrow, he drops his backpack and stands up perfectly straight.

Mark's not here, he says, not on this flight. I ran into this Marshall kid at breakfast, told him where we're going, and he just handed me a wad of cash the size of my fist in order to get on this expedition. Then he asked specifically not to be included in the dangerous parts of it. If Mark was here, I'd sit this kid on his lap to get him where he wants to go.

But there's no room left—

Remember all the times I've told you to let me take care of things? This is another one of them.

I walk back to my seat by the gate, and then the kid takes out both his earphones and turns to me again.

He asks, Are you going to Everest with Ray?

Yeah, I say.

Oh, he says, I'm Marshall Warren.

He extends his hand and I take it.

Bullshit, I say.

Excuse me?

You're Marshall Warren? Bullshit.

No, he says, I am.

Of Warren Technologies?

That's my father, Marshall Warren Jr. I'm the third. But I'm sure I'll work there too. Be CEO one day. That sort of thing.

That sort of thing? You mean being in charge of a huge computer manufacturer?

Yeah, he says.

With a hundred thousand employees?

Something like that.

My grandfather's Warren typewriter is still in my parents' basement, I say. My whole company uses Warren 896 desktops.

That's cool, he says.

What are you doing here?

Traveling. I graduated college last spring and I've been on the move ever since. I got to Nepal about a week ago and thought it'd be cool to see Mt. Everest up close.

Not to climb it?

I've never climbed a mountain, he says. I don't even really want to. It's dangerous. I do want to head up the company in a few years.

That sort of thing, I say.

Yeah, he says.

We fly in a twenty-seater twin engine to Lukla, a town which now serves mostly as a starting point for trips into the Khumbu region of the Himalayas. Basically, Everest tourism. It's an eight-day hike to Base Camp, including two days off at small towns for acclimatization to the altitude.

The group lands late in the day and spends the night in a hostel. We hardly see Lukla at all except for walking around to find dinner. I go to a noodle place near the hostel, and don't take any time to wander after I finish eating. All of us meet the next morning before sunrise and set off.

Once the sun gets above the peaks and my coffee kicks in, I see the range of glaciated mountains we're heading towards. They're so huge it looks like we should reach them by the end of the day.

We walk single file for the most part. At times people walk abreast and chit chat, but the group seems to have as much trouble acclimatizing to the new social setting as to the new altitude. Maybe it's because of the altitude. Ray walks first, and the Sherpa porters we've hired always walk behind us.

For a hundred dollars, a Sherpa will carry your equipment to Base Camp, and that money feeds his family for about six months. If he gets in three trips each year during the climbing season he's doing great. I knew this before I came, but it's still strange to hand over an average ATM withdraw to someone who considers it a half year's worth of wages.

Marshall struggles a little with the altitude on the first day. We all walk slower than we would at a lower elevation, but he walks at the end of our line, just ahead of the Sherpas. I hang back to help him out, which makes me wonder how in the last year or so I've become some sort of friend to every young person I meet. I hope I do a better job here than I did with Rayanne.

Take some of this, I say as I give him the bottle of Diamox that Mark made me buy before we left the States.

What is it? he asks as he takes out his white earphones.

It's supposed to help with altitude sickness, I say, ought to get you through the day.

Have you taken these? he asks.

Not yet, I say.

I walk with him for the rest of the first day. I see a few people chatting, and they look back at the two of us, I imagine because they're wondering about Marshall—I don't think anyone else besides Ray has had a conversation with him. He keeps those earbuds in while he hikes, even while right next to me. I hear a little white noise coming out of them, but can't make out what it is. I wonder how much of this he's taking in because the wind through the valley and the way it gently rustles the branches is half of what keeps me grounded here. Sometimes no music is better.

And then there are the banyan and pipal trees lining our trail. I've never really seen them before. The pipals have huge, thick canopies compared to those white ashes I read under in the Poconos, and I think that it's no wonder Siddhartha is said to have been under one when he was first enlightened. The banyans have sinewy trunks, like five or six smaller trees tied together at the roots and woven upward.

I think about the bamboo forests I hiked through in Japan, and the waves of green that make up the New England forests. This is cooler.

But then I find myself twenty yards ahead of Marshall and I hang back again. I consider telling him to give it a few minutes without his headphones, maybe asking a little about why he wants to shut out part of the experience here, but I don't. Even if we don't talk, he seems to do better when I'm right next to him.

I haven't got it today, but I will, that feeling that I'm alone, that it's me and the mountain. Get to the top and get down. It's only day one.

The group hikes for four hours on the first day, stays at a boarding house which stands alone on the side of the trail, then goes six hours the next day until we reach Namche Bazaar, a mountainside village where we're going to acclimatize. Since we're at 11,000 feet, twice the elevation of Denver, the whole expedition is exhausted.

The next day we have no schedule, so I sleep late and then go out into Namche. Less than a thousand people live here all year round, and the whole town has a strange blue tint to it. It takes me a little while to notice, but all the buildings have a blue trim on them, on the shutters, on the roofs. The people are dressed in all sorts of colors, but the place appears azure at every turn. When I walk close to the edge of town, which takes about ten minutes from our little hotel, I see a snow-capped peak rising up just across the valley. It looks like it's leaning towards Namche, threatening to devour it.

There must be four or five other expeditions in Namche on their way to some mountain in the Khumbu region— Everest, Lhotse, Makalu—and we all slide past each other in the outdoor markets and fight for seats at the internet cafe. When I get my time I write to Lisa about that peak above the town, and send a quick note to Mark about where we are.

I pass almost everyone in my expedition at some point during the day, and we say hello, talk for a few minutes, but then go our own ways. I see Marshall once, and he seems to be chatting with a local merchant.

The next day when we resume our hike I ask him if he speaks any Nepali.

Nope, he says.

We walk away from Namche for about an hour before Ray taps me on the shoulder and points to the peaks in the distance.

I ask, What?

What do you think?

It takes a few seconds, but then I recognize it from the pictures: Mt. Everest, flanked by the almost as massive peaks of Lhotse and Nuptse. The summit pyramid isn't the highest thing on the horizon from this perspective, and at our distance I can only fill in details from the photographs I remember. But that's it. I have a point to focus on, the top of something I can see. Get up, get down.

Over the next two days of hiking, the expedition members begin to get a little tighter. We still don't talk much while on the move, though everyone including Marshall has acclimatized well, but at night we start opening up—maybe because we're not so exhausted as we were the first few days, maybe because we realize that if we want human interaction for the next month, this is it.

So I end up in a playful argument with Alex, the Scottish climber, about whether Hüsker Dü is better than Bob Mould's later band, Sugar. He's five years older than me, and prefers the original band. I insist that Sugar is when everything in the music finally clicked.

The four climbers from the Western United States— Colorado, Utah, California and Washington—trade stories about the Rockies, while the two Canadians from Alberta argue that their northern segment of the range has the better climbs.

We ask no personal questions. We keep the conversations light and don't take ourselves seriously. The Americans ask the Canadians if they made their trekking poles out of old hockey sticks. They ask us how we keep our hamburgers fresh in our backpacks. We all ask Ray what it's like being an Aussie, which like every Kiwi he hates. He never responds with anything except a forced smile, but the group keeps at him—it's funnier knowing he hates it.

Marshall is the only one who stays on the outskirts. He keeps ahead of the Sherpas now, but when we get to the inns where we spend the nights he stays quiet at dinner and then goes to his room. I want to knock on his door just to ask how he is, but with how exhausted I am he must be asleep the moment he lies down. He seems fine every morning, so I don't mention anything about it.

The expedition takes its second acclimatization day in Dingboche, a village even smaller than Namche and with nothing to do except rest or wait in line to use the single phone booth. I make my call to Lisa short and tell her about how beautiful it is up here, that the other people are pretty cool. She tells me that she misses me, that she resents having to take the garbage out while I'm gone, and that the cats are no help with anything. Because…they're cats.

She asks, Has Mark caught up to you yet?

No.

He's the only one I trust to watch over you, she says. He makes it through all sorts of crazy things.

I've traveled plenty. Mostly with you, in case you've already forgotten.

We've spent more time in international subway systems than foreign parks. Let me know as soon as he catches up with you guys.

That afternoon we all bring our lunches to a little stream just outside town. Marshall comes with, but he sits about twenty-five yards away from the rest of us and listens to his iPod.

After we all eat I decide that I finally have to talk to him and walk over, jumping from rock to rock to avoid the cold stream.

Hey, I say, you want to come hang out with us?

No thanks, he says as he pulls out his earbuds.

You all right with the way everything's going so far?

Yeah, he says.

Then he turns his head away from me and stares pensively at the stream.

He says, Makes me think of my freshman year philosophy class.

What, I say, about Heraclitus?

Yeah. Wow, how'd you know that?

Philosophy by a stream, it's got to be Heraclitus: you can't step into the same river twice.

I thought I was the only one left who read about stuff like that.

My wife studies philosophy, I say, she gives me the good stuff. But it's a small club, we should have jackets made.

Well, anyway, I was just thinking about that line while I ate.

It means that change is constant, I say. But look at where you are, this village has been the same for thousands of years, they don't even have indoor plumbing except for the hostels.

Maybe it's all college bullshit, Marshall says.

There is a lot of bullshit in college.

Seems to me like it was all bullshit.

Yeah, it seems that way now, but I'm sure you got a few good things from it. A couple good books if nothing else.

OK, he says, a couple.

We all know you learn to do your job on the job, not in class. That must really be the case for you. I don't suppose there were any megacorporation classes.

No, he says, none.

So after you graduated you came out here?

Landed in London and made my way East.

Alone the whole time?

Yeah. I told my dad I wanted to take a year off before I started working with him.

Wish I'd done something like that. Is it as cool as it sounds?

Um, he says, so far, yeah. By the way, is your friend the one who stayed in Kathmandu?

He is.

Is he all right?

He'll be fine, I say. Ray talked to him this morning. He's trying to find a way to get up here and meet us in a week or so.

That'll be nice.

I don't know what you're going to do when he gets here, I say.

We'll figure something out, he says.

I hope so.

The next morning we leave for Base Camp.

24
BASE CAMP

Base Camp looks as though a bored titan threw a few thousand boulders at the side of the range, and the shattered pieces then rolled down to form a moraine of rocks and light snow. The first thing you notice, surprisingly, is not the tallest mountain in the world, but the Khumbu icefall, a river of house-sized blocks of ice which looks like it will roll into Base Camp at any minute.

After it doesn't you crane your neck and arch your back to see the Everest massif. The Nepalese in camp call it Sagarmatha—Head of the Sky—which might be accurate for the people who see it every day. A name I think works better for the Western visitor is Impales the Sky. The Comcast Center, the Tokyo Tower, the Gherkin are all tenements to me now.

The camp itself is the most colorful thing we've seen in days—lines of red, blue, yellow and orange tents against the gray rubble terrain at the bottom of the mountains. The smaller tents are mostly domes fit for two or three people, and each expedition has theirs together in a row or cluster. Then there are the big tents that look like barns made out of aluminum poles and Gore-Tex. Some of those are for dining, some for medicine. There are three doctors in Base Camp to attend to anything they can when someone gets hurt, and unless this year's the exception, they'll have plenty of work.

If you want it, you can get a 3G connection in one of the big tents, and high speed wifi in a few of them. Within an hour of arriving I see a dozen people carrying laptops and iPads around.

I'm starting to understand all the critics of Everest tourism. It looks like the people here are more concerned with blogging their climb than doing it right.

Ray gives everyone in the Peak Seekers expedition two days to rest our sore shoulders and crackling knees before we start training for the climb to the summit. We sleep late and eat a lot. I finish reading The Innocents Abroad, get through all of Choke in one evening, and start Citadel on the Mountain.

The different expeditions in camp mingle the best they can through the language barriers. A group of South American climbers who arrived a few days before us go around one afternoon and offer everyone gourds full of mate tea. I take it and look at the stuff, which resembles an algae covered pond, but try it anyway. It's incredible, like green tea but with the accent of a wood fire. East coast winters would be a lot better if Starbucks served this stuff instead of Frappuccinos. I share the drink with them and we all smile, but they don't speak English and I took Latin in high school.

Marshall and I share a tent. He's an easy roommate, keeps everything neat, folds all his clothes and puts them back in his bag when he gets undressed at night, and does the same in the morning with what he slept in. He wanders the camp during the day, and seems to sit near other people's conversations. I rarely see him talking to anyone else, but he's never just by himself either.

He walks around like he owns the camp. He doesn't act that way or say anything obnoxious, it's just his gait, his posture, the way his jacket seems to never wrinkle when he sits and his blonde hair stays in place even under a wool hat. He's not like us, he's made of something better, and I may think that all the more because I'm sure he'd never see himself that way.

The second day in camp, after dinner I see him outside our tent, crouched down.

You OK?

I have this headache, he says. I've been taking ibuprofen all day but I can't get rid of it. Do you think I have altitude sickness?

Maybe, I say. How much water have you been drinking?

I don't know, a normal amount I guess.

You need more, I say, a lot more. The air here, it's so dry it dehydrates you as much as a hundred degree day. Try drinking two or three bottles before bed and see how you feel tomorrow.

Cool.

The next morning I wake up as Marshall unzips the tent to go get breakfast and I ask how he's feeling.

Great, he says, best morning since we got here.

Nice, I say. Then I get ready for training.

Ray starts our climbing exercises to get us ready for the ascent. He gets us on icy rocks and steep trails to see how we'll handle the rigors of the climb and higher altitudes. He teaches us all how he wants a piton driven into rock or ice, if we need it, and how to properly thread the ropes. He says that if we get confused to call him, or one of the two Sherpas that will climb with us. Mostly, though, he drives us on, tries to toughen us up.

Imagine sweating while your fingers freeze, and air that takes more energy to suck in than it gives your lungs. Think about the moisture from your breath freezing on the edge of your beard, the one you're growing not to keep warm but because you're too tired to shave. That's our first few days of training.

And I feel like I raise my game because of it.

I'm one of the first to finish each hike and get to the top of each wall. My crampons begin to feel like extensions of my feet, and sometimes when I grab on to holds I forget that I'm wearing gloves.

I feel the altitude, the fight to breathe a little more deeply and get that extra oxygen, but I manage it.

Climbing here never gets easy, it's not supposed to, but it does go from being a struggle to something more like instinct and muscle memory. That's how you want it when your brain capacity diminishes with each hour of ascent to the summit.

I find that I'm always with people. The rest of the expedition on training climbs, long dinner tables, Marshall in our tent. The only chance I have to be alone, to look at the mountain and think about what I'm about to do, is at dusk. The place quiets down some, probably because people are eating dinner and exhausted, and when the sun sinks behind the range all the lights go on in the tents so they look like a series of Chinese lanterns placed reverently at the foot of Everest. The sky is darker than the peaks, so I walk to the edge of camp, just out of its glow, and look up for a few minutes at what I want to do. The clutter in my brain begins to recede. The ice and snow start raising a wall between me and the rest of camp as I stare at that rock. But the solitude only ever lasts a moment, there's always a group laughing as they leave the mess tent, someone carrying oxygen and letting the bottles clang together—something to keep me from being totally alone there. I haven't gotten it yet, but I will.

One evening an early and successful expedition comes back into Base Camp and tells us about how one of their members had collapsed in the Death Zone, the final stage of the climb where the air is so thin that it's impossible to survive for more than a day or so. I guess no one's ever too tired to hear about a near fatality, and we all crowd around to listen, or watch, really.

The group speaks German, but tells us what happened with gestures we all understand. People shout questions at them in a half dozen languages, and I can't help but join in.

Marshall, as usual, sits on the fringe of the group, quiescent, observing.

I find him later on by the tent. He's standing up and writing in a journal while using a huge rock with a level surface as a desk. He's under the light of an electric lantern, with his earbuds in, and has a mug of Sherpa tea balanced next to his journal. The Sherpas use yak butter and salt in their tea instead of milk and sugar. We've all taken to the South Americans' mate, but no one besides Marshall can stand that Sherpa stuff.

He sees me, then puts his pen down and takes out his earphones. He says, I'm leaving soon.

Really? Are you going home?

Maybe. I don't know, it depends on what I see tonight.

What are you doing tonight?

Staying up and watching the sunrise.

Is that what you came up here for?

Yeah, he says. Well, maybe. I hope.

All right, I say.

He looks down at his mug, then sees his journal lying open on the rock and shuts it.

What are you writing about? I ask.

Nothing important. Just keeping a record.

OK, I say.

He says, Do you mind if I ask why you're here?

Same reason as everyone, I say, to climb the mountain.

No, that's not what I mean. Why do you want to climb it?

That's what my wife asks me. It's hard to say, really, but I'm here more or less because it's worthless.

What? he asks.

It's not easy to explain, I say.

Would you mind trying?

I have, a few times, but it never seems to be clear. I guess it's that I grew up with all my grade school and high school teachers telling everyone that they could do incredible things with hard work. My parents were the same way. They're still that way, actually, always telling me that I can do something important. They never told me that I might not want to do anything important.

I begin wondering why I feel so comfortable telling him all this.

What do you do? he asks.

I'm the regional manager of a cable hardware distributor.

And you don't find that satisfying?

It's fine, I say. But it's not an important job. I didn't think it would be. I never wanted to change the world, I never thought I could. And climbing this mountain, it changes nothing at all. It's totally useless to anyone.

Except you, he says.

Yeah, I say, except me.

He says, Your wife must be pretty cool to let you do something like this.

She is.

What's she like?

Like me, I say. She's never happier than in a quiet room with a cup of coffee and a book. She loves traveling, too. We make a good couple.

Any kids?

Not yet, I say. Probably when we get back. She's at that point. We never talked about it much, and then a few months ago she got baby crazy. It seemed like it happened overnight to me.

Are you at that point?

I don't know, I say, are men ever at that point? The best piece of wisdom my dad ever gave me was that he wanted to have kids when my mom told him he wanted to have kids.

OK...

It just means good dads sometimes have to get dragged into it. My parents are crazy hippies, but they were good parents.

So, he says, this is your last adventure before kids?

I'd feel pretty bad risking my life for something useless when I have a kid at home.

Marshall tilts back his cup and finishes his tea.

That's all pretty cool, he says.

It's a little strange to say out loud, I tell him. All this time and money for something completely unproductive.

I think I get it, he says. Besides, it's your time and money. Do what you want with it.

Thanks. So, why are you here?

To see the sunrise.

OK, I say, if we're opening up, I don't buy that you're just up here to see the sights. I knew rich kids in college, and they didn't travel like you do. They stayed at nice hotels in big cities, they went in groups, they got hammered all the time, and they said they got laid. They said so a lot, they couldn't stop talking about where they went and who they banged over spring break or summer vacation. You're a loner, I get that, but you could be by yourself in any hotel or restaurant in the world, and

226   JOSHUA ISARD

instead you're out here with us, sharing dirty toilets and freeze dried food in the middle of nowhere. I'd understand it if you were climbing, one of those risk taking CEOs, but all you do is meander and listen to music. I haven't seen you embracing any part of being out here, and I just can't figure out why you came.

Marshall exhales hard. He leans his elbows against the rock, lets it take his whole weight.

Did you ever study the Holocaust? he asks.

Not really, I say. I'm more of a cultural Jew.

I didn't know you were Jewish.

Yeah. I thought the mass of curly hair gave it away.

Not really. But then you especially would know about World War II, right?

Maybe lapsed Jew is a better way to put it.

All right, he says. Anyway, I took this class during my last semester about the Holocaust, and the moment that sticks out most in my mind is when our professor told us that after the Nazis burned people in the camps' crematoriums they sold the ashes to local farmers. The farmers didn't only know what they bought, but fought for it because it did wonders for the crops.

Fucking hell, I say.

Yeah, that's not what I thought. I didn't think anything, or feel anything in my gut. I just wrote the fact down in my notebook like it was the next line in a geometry proof. My friends gasp over celebrity breakups and scream after touchdown passes, but me, well, not even the Nazis phase me.

So, I say, the Himalayas then? It's pretty dramatic.

Now it's the Himalayas, he says. First it was the Lake District, then Rome, then the fjords, then the Ganges…you get the idea.

I do.

I just want to react to something, he says. I've never seen mountains without a resort built on them, and tomorrow morning I'm going to get up before dawn to watch the sun roll over those peaks. I don't know what I'm going to feel, since apparently I don't feel much, but I hope it's something. And if it is, I'll go home.

After the one moment?

I'm a business man, he says, not a yogi. It just sucks to be so cold, to not connect with anything. So I'd like to show myself at least once that I'm not like that.

Yeah, I say, that would be good.

Marshall opens his journal back up and scribbles something down, then rips out the page and holds it up.

Look, he says, here's my email address. When you get home, get in touch with me. Maybe I can find a place for you at the company.

Thanks, but I've only got a communications degree. My job the way it is doesn't require anything beyond common sense.

That's a pretty rare trait, he says. It'd be nice to work with someone I can trust to help me out, show me a few management things.

Really, thanks, but my company's not in the same league as your dad's.

Hey, I'm not starting as CEO. Besides, people are people, in any office. I don't know that Warren Technologies will be any more fulfilling for you, but it probably pays more.

I do all right.

Yeah, well, I'll bet my dad can make sure you do better.

OK, I say as I take the paper from him. Thanks.

No problem.

25
SNOW DRIFTS

The next morning the tent is warmer than usual so I stay in my
sleeping bag longer than I have since we got here. I'm tired and
stiff from the few days of climbing exercises we've had, but
Ray was right: with all the training before we left the fatigue
and sore muscles aren't so bad.

A warm tent, though…I haven't had that yet.

I look around and see that Marshall's not in here, but all
his stuff is. He hasn't left. He must still be out watching the
sun or already in the mess tent.

I prop myself up on my elbows and think about how much
it must suck to have to go around the globe looking for feeling. I
never emote or anything, but I love my wife, I'm punched in the
gut at the end of A Farewell to Arms, I panicked a little when I
once thought Virginia had gotten out and was wandering the city
streets until I found her in a dark corner of our building's hallway.

Did his dad do something to make him that way?
Billionaire, probably always in meetings, putting his family in
a house so cavernous they could go days without seeing each
other. That might make a person a little cold.

Or he read something. Camus is probably still popular in
college courses. Too much of that will take it out of you.

I never thought I'd feel bad for a crazy rich kid, but I do
and I hope he figures it out.

As I pull myself out of my sleeping bag I start thinking about why it's warmer. No one predicted any change in temperature, a serious weather front that might cause this. It should be colder. I get dressed, wind my watch, and look forward to the coffee they'll have brewed at the mess tent by now.

Then I unzip the tent and get knocked back on my ass by the snow that pours in. I think that it must be a joke, but no one on our expedition seems like a prankster, and if another group piled up snow just to laugh as I fall and my gear gets wet I'd be pretty pissed off.

It's bright and clear outside, but once I dig out I find myself in four feet of snow. There's a drift right up against my tent, and all the others in our group. I wade around and see that the other side of the tent is only covered a quarter of the way, and that there's actually about a foot of snow on the ground.

The drift was enough to provide insulation.

I half walk, half hop through the snow to the mess tent, which is functioning as usual. I grab a cup of coffee and sit down across from Ray who is the only other person in here.

Shit, I say, that must have been a hell of a storm last night.

It's nothing when you're down here, he says. Just be glad you weren't at Camp III, or on the South Col. Up that high people die when the winds get like that.

Was anyone up there? I ask.

No, he says. There was a group at Camp I, but they're fine. They radioed in a few hours ago.

I can't believe I slept through that, I say, it made a drift on our tents up to my elbows.

I know, he says, I saw.

Ray sips his coffee and turns his head back to the magazine

he was reading before I showed up. I'm sure he's seen worse than what happened last night, but he doesn't care that we haven't.

What did Marshall think? Ray asks.

Beats me, I say, he wasn't in the tent when I got up.

Where is he?

I don't know. He wanted to go out early and watch the sunrise, I actually thought he might be here by now.

What? Ray says as he drops his magazine to the table.

It's a long story, I say, but Marshall really wanted to see the sun rise over the mountains. He told me all about it—

Ray cuts me off and says, He went out of the tent last night...and he's not back or in here.

He gets up and runs to the door, then charges out into the snow. He's screaming the names of everyone else in camp that he knows.

Mesí! Tremblay! He yells, Van der Brook! Jackson! Get up, now!

I'm running after him but can't catch him. When he pauses for a breath I yell, Ray! What is this?

Ray turns and says, Are you an idiot? This storm hit just before dawn, Marshall was out in it last night.

I think, Fuck.

The quick zips of tents opening fill the camp for a moment—half-dressed climbers begin to appear from every expedition.

Just start looking for him, Ray says to me.

Then he gallops to the tents and tells everyone else what they're looking for.

Base Camp looks a lot softer than it did the day before. The snow covered so many of the rocks that only the biggest boulders breach the surface, and most of those are covered on one side by a drift. There are no plows, no kids with sleds, no telephone poles with wires you're worried might snap and leave you in a blackout until whenever. It strikes me how rarely, in the city or the suburbs, we have a chance to see snow the way it lies.

And here the scene only lasts a few minutes, because everyone gets up and kicks through it, looking for Marshall.

At first I rush ahead with everyone else, calling his name, hoping he found a little shelter and fell asleep in the cold. Maybe he'll only lose a few fingers, some toes. Then I stop to think for a minute and everyone else bolts past me, kicking up clouds of snow crystals as they go.

I scan the area for where he would have gone. I know what I'm looking for, what he would have looked for. And it takes me a while but I see it, a boulder rising above the snow, one with a flat surface where you could rest a journal.

I wade through the snow and the other people. It's strange, but with the sun out on a clear morning like this one most people get hot quickly. They take off their jackets, toss them on the snow, and search in t-shirts and heavy snow pants, always adjusting their suspenders as they walk. The men brush the snow off their beards, the women shake it out of their hair. I trudge along past them, unzip my jacket, but don't take it off.

The boulder I see is only barely within ear shot of the group. None of them seem to think he would have gone this far, and they don't see me walk past, or they don't care. As I approach the rock their voices fade and all I hear is my boots crunching through the snow, the wisping as I leave billows of white dust behind me.

Marshall's not at the boulder. I kick the snow away from

the sides, dig down to the gravel, but he's not there. If he was lying flat, the snow would cover him completely, and if he was sitting up we'd see him against the white background. I start walking around the area, scanning the surface of the snow for any color, thinking of the next logical place to look.

Then my boot crunches something different—definitely not a stone. It breaks under my sole.

I drop to my knees and dig with my hands until a white cord gets tangled around my fingers. It's Marshall's earbuds. I scoop the snow to the side with both hands, like I'm doing the breaststroke, and then I scratch against Marshall's jacket. His iPod is right next to his arm, and for some reason I stuff it in my pocket as I shovel the snow away. I clear the area around his head because, even though I already know he's dead, you have to check for the miracle.

He's frozen. His eyelids are blue with blood crystals; his lips are so dry and chapped they split in thirty places; the tip of his nose is black with frostbite. He has a gash running from his temple to the middle of his cheek.

I want to call for help, but everyone else is a football field away, and I'm not sure they'll hear me. I can't hear them.

Before I try, I look at Everest. There's no wind, no sound at all. It's me and the mountain. Its straight lines, its apathy to my presence. The clear goal: get up, get down. There is nothing else.

Except the body right next to me.

And instead of anything else I think: did he feel something the way I do right now?

I scream for help, that I found him. I scream so hard that I break out in a fit of coughing as the Himalayan air sucks all the moisture out of my throat. I try to get up but fall backwards. They're coming, I can hear their boots in the snow. From the ground I yell again that he's here, right here next to me.

Ray shows up first, then some of the South Americans. He looks down at me and I shake my head back and forth. He checks, but he knows.

I stand up and turn around to find that nearly the whole camp has arrived and formed a semicircle around Marshall. They look at me and I feel like I'm supposed to say something. Instead I shoulder my way through them and walk towards my tent. I grip Marshall's iPod in my pocket the whole way.

This is what Marshall Warren most probably did on the morning he went to watch light break on the Himalayas:

As planned, he got up before sunrise and went outside. He saw flurries falling. The wind gusted irregularly, sending the snowflakes horizontal for a few seconds each time. This is nothing unusual at Base Camp. He took a flashlight, a thermos of Sherpa tea, his journal, and his iPod to that flat boulder away from the tents where he sat and waited for the sun to rise. He was not stupid about this. He wore extra layers because pre-dawn is the coldest time of day, and even brought chemical warming packets for his gloves and boots.

Everyone agrees that he took the proper precautions for what he wanted to do.

The thing is that anyone anywhere near Everest is by necessity a weather junkie, though knowing the reports is not the same as knowing for sure what the weather will be. Marshall knew "light snow overnight, clearing up before morning" and must have figured that he was in the last vestiges of precipitation.

What happened was one of those things meteorologists say they can't predict, as if the mountains conspired to move a front so that the clouds ripped open on a peak and dumped a blizzard in minutes.

Marshall must have expected that calm morning for too long. When he realized what was going on and tried to make it back to the tents, which are brightly colored for a moment just like this one, he lost his way. Visibility, they estimate, was three feet, and the wind would have shot snow into his eyes when he tried to open them. His flashlight wouldn't have helped at all. He never could have seen the colored Gore-Tex.

Marshall walked in the wrong direction.

From the gash and scrapes on the side of his face we figure that he tripped, was knocked unconscious, and died of exposure. The wound hardly bled, it froze over so fast.

I stay in my tent all day playing with Marshall's iPod, which starts working once it thaws out a little. There's almost entirely classical music on it: Schubert, Rachmaninoff, Berlioz. Names I've heard of but never listened to. I plug my headphones into it and click through the tracks one by one, artist by artist, never listening to one for more than thirty seconds or so. I've always felt a little uncultured because of this, but after Beethoven's Fifth and the 1812 Overture I don't know a thing about classical music, and I've never cared to learn.

Ray brings me a sandwich at lunchtime and says he wants to get the whole group out for a light climb in an hour. He says it's important to keep moving, that these things happen every year and they're no one's fault.

I tell him that I'm not really up for it.

He says that most of the other expeditions are already

training today. He tells me it's not disaffection, that death is a reality here and climbers deal with it the best way they can, by climbing. He says that's the best way to honor Marshall.

I tell Ray that Marshall didn't even want to summit the mountain, that all he wanted to see was a sunrise, and that I don't see how getting to the top of a big rock honors anything.

He says he understands, claps me on the shoulder, and leaves.

I keep clicking through Marshall's music the rest of the day and looking at his things on the other side of the tent, which is small enough that I can reach over and touch his bag, his shirts, his pillow without moving from my sleeping bag. I don't, though. The most I do is toss his crushed earbuds into the corner so I can't see them anymore.

Then, at dusk, Mark shows up at the tent. He unzips it a little, pops his head in to say hello, and then I crawl out to see him.

Holy shit, he says, what happened up here?

We shake hands and do the man-hug thing where we pound our fist on the other's back.

How did you get here? I ask.

I hitched on with four Swedes who came up to do some geology research. This place is strange, everyone seems exhausted. When I asked where our tents are no one said anything, they just pointed over here.

You showed up on the wrong day, I say and then tell him about Marshall, about the trek up here and what happened this morning.

Wait, he says, Marshall Warren, the computer mogul?

His son, I say.

Oh my god, Mark says, that's unbelievable. Is the expedition still on?

Yeah, I say, they trained this afternoon.

I take one of his packs and we go into the tent so he can put everything down.

Shit, he says and then slumps down on Marshall's sleeping bag.

That was his stuff, I say.

Mark jumps up. He says, Oh.

I'll ask Ray what to do with it.

The next morning I hear Mark leave the tent early. I peek out as he's zipping up the flap and see that the sky is still the color of deep ocean water so I go back to sleep.

I get up when it's bright out, get dressed, wind my watch. Marshall's pack is gone, replaced by Mark's, the way it should have been. Then I look at my things—my messed up sleeping bag, little pillow, books thrown to the corner of the tent, half empty pack lying on its side. It won't take long to get it all together.

Mark comes in with a cup of coffee, looks at me and says, What are you doing?

Packing, I say. I'm going home.

What? he says. Why?

I guess I got what I came here for.

Is this because of Marshall Warren?

Yeah, I say. Pretty much.

You have to let it go, he tells me. It's like Ray said, it's the reality of things here, it's no one's fault.

I don't think it's my fault, I say, I just want to leave now.

Nathan, come on, you have to tough this one out. Ray

and I took all his stuff over to the mess tent this morning, you won't have to see anything of his to remind you. And you're here, at the foot of the mountain, you can't go now.

I got what I came here for, I say.

Wait, he says, let's talk about this a minute. I mean, you said you didn't want any sort of spiritual thing—

You touch any corpses this week? I ask.

Mark gets quiet now.

Listen to a dead guy's music?

Are you afraid now? he asks. I'd understand if you were.

Not really, I say, but I think I know that this isn't where I ought to be.

Mark doesn't put up any more of a fight, and backs away from me just a few inches. He must see that the connection between me and this mountain, which I've had since I was a kid in the Poconos scrambling up those peaks and imagining myself as a great explorer, has broken.

26
FEEDBACK AND APATHY

I have to wait at Base Camp for another day before I find
a group going back to Kathmandu—a few people from an
Italian expedition who got altitude sickness at Camp III and
couldn't go any higher without risking edema or a hemorrhage.
They don't speak English and I don't know a word of Italian,
so I basically trail them along the route.

At Gorak Shep, the first little settlement below Everest
Base Camp—really just a collection of a half dozen buildings
to serve mountaineers—I call Lisa and tell her everything that
happened.

You're OK? she asks.

Yeah.

It was really Marshall Warren's kid?

Yes.

Oh my god, she says.

I think that I'm going to hear these exact questions for a
month after I get home.

She says, I could smack you.

Still?

All that time and money to not climb a mountain.

You want me to go back up there?

No, she says. No. Nathan, I love you, just come home, I
want you to come home.

But you could smack me?

Lovingly, she says.

On the way back we stay in the same towns, at the same boarding houses. We see other expeditions, but all on their way up to Base Camp—there's still plenty of time left in the climbing season. Without needing acclimatization days we're on a flight to Kathmandu in less than a week, and from there I book a seat on the next flight back home. I don't leave the airport, even though I have to sleep in the terminal because my plane doesn't start boarding for another ten hours.

During the eighteen hours of travel time, fifteen in the air and a layover in Frankfurt, I click though tracks by PJ Harvey, Smashing Pumpkins, Jane's Addiction. I've always thought that you can't use music to change your mood, that you ought to find something that goes with how you feel. Catherine Wheel, Leonard Cohen…I can't find anything depressing enough.

When they darken the cabin and all I have for illumination is the reading light which I'm sure annoys the woman next to me, I let my mind wander. I think about the girl in middle school who had cancer and came to class wearing a bandana for two years as she got thinner, paler, more frail, until her skin was like shrink wrap and she died. I remember my freshman year at Montcrief when someone living in my dorm jumped off the roof and landed right in front of the main entrance. I'd never met him, but I still used the back door for the next few weeks.

Then I think about Marshall's face, broken and scarred, like the cold and wind were wild animals scavenging his flesh after he died.

I don't sleep on either flight.

Lisa picks me up from the airport, and knocks the bags out of my hands when she jumps at me as I leave customs. She drives home the whole way in the left lane with the windows down, the cool evening air of late spring whipping her hair around and cutting across my face. It's loud enough that we can't hear the radio, and we don't talk.

Once we're parked in our garage we decide that lugging my bags in can wait until morning, so we just walk upstairs to go to sleep. I'm about to go into our bedroom when I notice that the spare room is finished. The walls are yellow, there's a bed against one wall, a dresser against another, and a small TV. Lisa's framed and hung a few pictures from our travels: one from Edinburgh, one from Andalucía, another from Osaka. There's a space near the door that I think would easily fit a crib and a changing table.

Looks good, I say as I walk in.

My dad came over and helped me build the furniture, Lisa says. It wasn't expensive, everything's from IKEA and my parents gave us the TV that was sitting in their den. Your mom helped me pick out the frames for the photos.

I walk over to the bed, which has a light blue blanket over it and white pillowcases. I fall down on it. I can smell myself and my musty clothes. My face is slippery with oil after flying for a full day. But I don't want to get up.

Lisa lies down with me and puts her arm over my shoulder. We take up the entire bed to the point that my shoulder is against the wall and her elbow is over the other edge. The cats still find spots, one between my feet and the other on the pillow next to Lisa's head.

That's how we fall asleep.

~

The hardest thing about coming home isn't that I have to talk about what happened—that's actually kind of cathartic. I tell Lisa and my parents everything, every detail about the frozen corpse to the point that my mother says to stop, so I ask her to leave the room while I finish the story for my dad. Over the first few days I'm back I add details for Lisa as they come to me: that I coughed all afternoon after screaming for help when I found the body; that while I walked back to the tent I thought I ought to fall in the snow or cry or something, but I didn't, I just trudged back; that I still have Marshall's iPod in my backpack sitting in our garage.

It's not hard lying to everyone else either. For weeks my coworkers and big clients ask what happened—when Marshall Warren Jr.'s kid dies, it's news. Did I meet him while I was there? Did I know what happened to him? I tell them I barely spoke with him, that I had to come down early because of AMS and, well, what can you do? Climbing's not worth dying over, is it?

When you tell a lie enough times you start to believe it. That might not be the best thing to do in the long run, psychologically, but it's working right now.

Even Alan Gillian asks if I'm OK. I see him pulling out of his driveway one morning while I take some bills out to the mailbox. Rayanne is in the backseat.

I heard about what happened over there, he says. Did you know that Warren boy?

Never met him, I say. I came down before all that.

Oh. Shame about it, though.

Yeah it is. How are you guys?

We're very well, Alan says, thank you.

How're you, Rayanne?

I'm all right, she says.

Cool, I say.

I don't tell either of them, or anyone for that matter, that when I see Rayanne she's often wearing her headphones—big ones, noise canceling headphones—and that at those moments I hear the crunch of Marshall's earbud under my boot every time.

It's not even hard to rest. The first few weeks I'm home, I laugh out loud as we lie in bed and catch up on the Modern Family and 30 Rock episodes I missed. Most nights I get a solid and uninterrupted eight hours of sleep.

Really, the only difficult thing I have to do to get back to normal is shave. I stopped shaving once we left Kathmandu, as did pretty much every other guy on an expedition, and so grew a decent beard by the time I got home. I figure out pretty quickly that razors are made for days of growth, not weeks, so I have to dig under the sink for Lisa's nail scissors and trim the best I can before shaving normally. Then I look in the mirror and see me from a few months ago. I've never skipped more than a day or two of shaving before this, so I could be looking at my reflection from high school, from the day Dan gave me that Pixies tape, from when I met Lisa, or the day we got married, or moved into this house.

Could be. But I'm not.

Mark got home yesterday and he's coming over here to tell me about everything. I know he summited. Two weeks after I got back he emailed me a picture of himself with his oxygen mask dangling at the side of his face, his cheeks red and raw from the cold, and his ice axe held over his head—Mark on the summit of Everest. I haven't heard from him since I left except for that picture.

When he shows up Mark takes my hand and then pulls me toward him to give me a full on hug. Then he pushes me back and slaps my shoulder, which hurts.

You OK? he asks.

Yeah. Congratulations on summiting.

Thanks.

We go into my kitchen and sit at the table with a few bottles of beer. The cats start attacking my shoelaces.

They must have missed you, he says.

No, I say. Lisa told me they took my side of the bed while I was gone and seemed pretty happy about it.

Oh.

Tell me about the climb.

We started for the summit ten days after you left, he says, and got back to Base Camp a week later. When we did, there were a dozen reporters waiting to talk about Marshall Warren's kid. They pretty much jumped Ray, asked him questions until he pushed through them and went back to his tent. Then they tried talking to everyone else in the expedition, and other people at the camp.

What did you guys say?

That's the thing, no one said anything. Well, nothing significant. Ray and a few other leaders gave this vague line about not remembering who exactly found the body, and that they thought the kid was nice but didn't know him well. Then everyone else did the same thing. Did you read any of the stories?

I didn't.

Oh, well, anyway, the day we were packing up to go back

to Lukla, Ray gets a call on the satellite phone from Marshall Warren asking about his son, and Ray won't tell him anything either. I mean, the guy just wants some closure, and Ray won't say a word except that he seemed like a really nice kid. You believe that? This magnate calls and Ray basically refuses to talk to him, says he knows nothing besides what's in the papers. Apparently he doesn't believe Ray and asks him to call later if he remembers anything.

I don't think Ray cares about that.

He's not going to call, Mark says, but he cares.

Then Mark slides an envelope across the table to me.

What's this? I ask.

Marshall Warren Jr.'s private phone number.

Are you serious? Ray told him about me?

No, Mark says, he just wanted to give you the number. In case you wanted to talk to him. About his son.

That's ridiculous.

Why?

I'm not calling Marshall Warren Jr., I say. I'm not calling one of the wealthiest computer magnates on Earth to talk about his dead kid.

No, Nathan, you're calling a father to talk about his son.

I don't think I have a lot to offer him, all right? Maybe this is better left alone right now.

Better for you?

Oh, come on. I'm fine, I'm not the guy who froze to death.

Exactly, Mark says. Think about it, though. Put yourself in this guy's position.

I don't really have anything in common with a tech billionaire.

He's just a dad right now. Like any dad.

I don't have anything in common with that either.

OK, Mark says, whatever you say.

It's a little chilly on my back patio. The spring breeze is strong, and late in the day it seems to send a message that we shouldn't get too excited, it isn't summer yet. I got home a half hour ago from a day of visiting two office managers and basically telling them how I would do their job differently. This isn't so far removed from what I did as a manager, I'm just doing it at a new office every few days. So far the Sirs like, as they say, the energy I've injected into the region. Whatever that means.

I'm wearing jeans and a hoodie, which is good enough to keep me comfortable today. I sit back and let the mug of green tea rest on my leg as I look at the needles and branches of my Norway spruces sway with the breezes. Above them the Harrisons' pin oak, still standing for now, seems hardly bothered by the wind.

When I finish the tea I go inside and then upstairs to the library where I scan the shelves for something to read. I don't feel like picking up something new, so I take out a collection of Flannery O'Connor and one of Raymond Carver, but I can't get into the stories of either one. I go older—The Sign of the Four—and then newer—Last Days of the Dog Men—but nothing works. I take my laptop into the library set iTunes to play random tracks: Longview, All Apologies, Outshined…I zone out in the middle of each one.

Lisa finds me in there when she comes home.

What's up hun? she says.

Nothing, I say.

That sounds like a loaded nothing.

I wish it was, but I can't concentrate on anything. Really, nothing's up.

Lisa leans over my chair and gives me a kiss on the forehead, then goes into the bedroom to change. I flip through my Pandora stations while I wait for her to come back. When she does she's wearing sweat pants and a tank top and asks if I'm ready for dinner soon.

Yeah, I say.

OK, she says, I'll start on it.

Then I go downstairs and out to the garage where I find my backpack and dig through it for Marshall's iPod. I bring it in and put it on the kitchen table, right next to the envelope Mark gave me yesterday.

What's that? Lisa asks while mixing something in a huge green bowl.

Marshall's iPod, I say.

She puts the bowl down and says, Why did you get it out?

Because I have Marshall Warren Jr.'s phone number.

I tell her what Mark told me about Ray not answering questions and sending the number home to me.

You have to call him, Lisa says.

Maybe I'll just send him the iPod, I say.

What good is that going to do?

You can tell a lot about a person by what's on their iPod.

That's not what a parent's interested in.

How would we know what a parent's interested in?

She says, Think about it for a minute. For someone who tries so hard not to to concern himself with other people you certainly managed to bring home a nice memento of someone you met. The least you can do now is spare some time to look inward.

What does that mean?

It means that you ought to take a long hard look at your personal philosophy of not letting anyone else into your life and how much it really applies anymore. Haven't you at all thought about having a child beyond when you're talking to me?

I have thought about it but I haven't told Lisa anything. I could go to Pixar movies in a few years without looking like a pedophile. I'd like to avoid baby talk all together—Lisa's got plenty of that ready, I imagine—and from the very beginning talk like an adult, even before my child utters a word. I've planned the kid's library, starting with William Shakespeare, Lewis Carroll, and Jack London—made an eighteen year long to-read list.

Nathan, Lisa says, that wasn't a rhetorical question.

Yes, I say, I have. I think about when the kid's old enough to ask about what it was like when we were kids, and I can tell her about the time when rock music had feedback and no one cared about anything.

Lisa laughs.

I say, What?

That's what you think about telling our child?

Yeah.

She gives me a hug, and while she still has her arms around me she says, You're going to be a good dad. Maybe not normal, but good.

Then she lets go and gives me a kiss. She looks at the iPod on the table for a few seconds and then goes back to her mixing bowl. I sit down at the kitchen table and watch her cook for a few minutes. It's like magic to me. Skillets, measuring cups, spices, meats and vegetables—I don't know what she does, but it seems choreographed, and in less than an hour it'll be dinner.

She's only just started.

I take the envelope and the iPod and walk upstairs to the library. I shut my laptop, put away all the books on my chair, and sit down. I wait for a few minutes, going over what I remember, the snow, the camp—I think about what the sun might look like rising over mountain tops and realize that I never saw that.

Then I call Marshall's dad.

It rings a few times before he picks up. Hi, I say, I wanted to talk to you about your son.

ACKNOWLEDGMENTS

Thanks especially to my family: to my wife, Kate, for her support as I stole time to write; to my parents Scott and Barbara, my brother Adam, and my Bubby, for always encouraging me; to Sylvia and Sia, my mascots; and to my daughter, Nora, who was a part of this well before she was born.

A special thanks for reading drafts of this book go to: Marshall Warfield, Beth Thorpe, and Genevieve Betts—band mates extraordinaire who reviewed chapter after chapter, revision after revision. Carlos Queirós—once again, you were right. Richard Wertime—you helped me turn the corner on a major issue, and how you found the time for that I'll never know.

I would not have gotten close to doing this without my esteemed pedagogues through the years: Lynn Caum, Barbara Macintosh, James Brown (The Godfather of Composition), Keith Gumery, Alan Jamieson, and Dilys Rose.

And finally, thanks to Lee Byrd, Bobby Byrd, John Byrd, and everyone at Cinco Puntos Press. You all put in so much work to make this the best book possible, and I hope you enjoyed the process as much as I did.